PIGGY

AN ORIGINAL NOVEL

PIGGY

THE CURE

by

TERRANCE CRAWFORD

and

DAN WIDDOWSON

Scholastic Inc.

© 2023 MiniToon Inc. Piggy & the Piggy characters, images, and logos are trademarks of MiniToon Inc. All Rights Reserved.

ISBN 978-1-338-84813-7

10 9 8 7 6 5 4 3 2 1   23 24 25 26 27

Printed in the U.S.A.   40

First printing 2023

Book design by Jeff Shake

PIGGY : THE CURE

On any normal day on the island city-state of Lucella, the sun would peek out from behind a cover of clouds, showering the island with golden rays. Dew-soaked blades of grass would sway lightly in the gentle breeze and the wind was so delicate that you couldn't tell where the air stopped and your skin began. On a normal day in Lucella, birds chirped merrily from the peaks of lush green treetops and the smell of the sea breeze wafted across the shore of the island. On a normal day, the laughter of Lucella's people echoed across the city, from the children outside a local schoolyard to the underground Metro station. On a normal day, there would be dozens of people milling around the city, going about their daily lives, just like anywhere else. Unfortunately, Lucella had not had a normal day in a very long time.

It had been months since the Infection had begun, the Infection that had caused perfectly normal people to begin acting . . . *strangely*. For reasons that were still unclear, several members of the population had been affected by something strange. Upstanding members of the community were suddenly growing bigger and more distorted, losing control of their bodies, becoming more aggressive, and sporting dull, glowing eyes. Those terrible eyes, they haunted Ben in his sleep, even now. That is, when he managed to get any sleep. Ben drew his jacket closer around his shoulders as he shuddered, trying to keep the thoughts of the things he had seen over the past few weeks at bay. Ben's friend Ollie shuddered as well, more worried about the future than the past.

Ben's whole journey had begun with Ollie; a weeks-long trek throughout the island to find him had led

them both here, to this very spot, outside a military base on the outskirts of town. The friends they had made along the way stood on the crest of the hill, watching over them, keeping alert for any sign of the encroaching Infected. Billy was an orange bull, much taller and larger than just about anyone that Ben had ever met. His dark gray horns, silver nose ring, and black spiked bracelet made him seem intimidating, but he was actually one of the sweetest people that Ben had ever met. Of course, it didn't hurt that he was as strong as an ox (even though he was a bull). Since they had met, Billy had carried around a large barbell. Whether it was an effort to keep fit, or simply a deterrent to the weaker Infected, Ben didn't know, and truthfully, he didn't care. Those weights and steel bar had already gotten them out of more than a few jams. Badgy, on the other hand, was . . . less personable. A white badger with a red tie, Badgy had spent most of their time together wisecracking, but Ben couldn't deny his usefulness in a fight. The glowing rod that he held close to him at all times had been proven to be just as effective a zombie deterrent as anything else they had come across, and Badgy wielded it with astonishing precision.

"*Ben.*" Ollie prodded gently, rousing Ben from his thoughts. "Are we doing this or not?" Ben looked at the door of the base and nodded resolutely. Of course they were doing this; they had come too far not to. Over the past few weeks, during their adventures across Lucella, they had been in infrequent contact via a police officer's walkie-talkie with a man who seemed to know more about this infection than he was letting on, and, if the helicopter parked outside this base was any indication, this was where that man had ended up. Ben took a deep breath to center himself, something he found himself doing more and more these days, then pulled the base door.

Nothing. The door didn't budge. Ben tried again, to no avail. Pushing, pulling, a series of rhythmic knocks, nothing seemed to work. "Wait a minute . . ." Ollie trailed off, moving to the side of the door. "There's a keypad here!" Ben moved to follow Ollie, grateful for a reason to take even a small break from trying to pry the door open. Ollie was right. On the side panel of the door, there was an old keypad, ten digits laid out on top of corresponding buttons and four digital blanks blinking almost mockingly at the duo.

"A four-digit passcode? We could be here all day trying out all of those!" Ben lamented, kicking a patch of dirt in frustration.

"Sure, that's one way to do it," Ollie started. Ben had known his friend long enough to recognize when he had a plan. "Or we could just use these four numbers." Ollie pointed at the keypad, and sure enough, four of the numbers had been worn down. "One, seven, four, and nine," said Ollie. "Those four numbers have been used more than the rest. We put those in the proper order . . ."

"We've got ourselves the code to the base." Ben finished his friend's thought. It was smart, something that would have taken Ben himself a lot longer to figure out. Ben punched the numbers into the keypad in order, only to be greeted by a red flashing light and a series of angry beeps. *Okay, so not in numerical order*, Ben thought to himself. "Well? Keep going, right? There's like . . . five thousand possible combinations of these numbers."

Ben quirked a brow as he put in the numbers again, this time in a different order. "How do you even know that?" he queried, the lights flashing red once more.

"It's . . . it's pretty basic binomial coefficient, right?" Ollie must have seen the expression on his friend's face. "You really didn't pay attention in math class, huh?" Ollie jabbed.

"Well, the last time I was in school . . ." Ben's words trailed off as he thought back to an earlier adventure, feeling a pang of guilt as he remembered Bunny and how she had most likely sacrificed her only chance at survival to help him get to the Metro station to save his friend. Bunny would be happy to know that her efforts were not in vain.

Ben was shaken from his reverie again as Ollie reached past him, inputting another series of numbers into the keypad. It seemed like hours, but truthfully, it was only a few minutes when Ollie entered the proper sequence into the keypad. With a rapidly blinking green light, the keypad chirped in approval, the heavy gray steel doors of the base parting slowly with a groan, a clear sign of disrepair. Ben wondered when the last time someone had been here was. "Well, would you look at that? Open sesame!" Ollie quipped, justifiably pleased with himself. The doors slid all the way open, sunlight flooding the cavernous opening of the base and revealing a set of stairs leading to a lower level. Ben turned back to look at Badgy and Billy, giving them a thumbs-up. Billy returned the gesture as well as he could, considering that most bulls did not have opposable thumbs. Ben could tell from here that Badgy was rolling his eyes, but he, too, returned the thumbs-up. The two old friends resumed their guard as Ollie met Ben's eyes.

"Are you ready for this?" Could anyone ever be ready for something like this? Ben nodded, and together the two descended the stairs, the metal doors whisking shut behind them. The doors shutting threw their surroundings into stark relief. Where minutes ago, the harsh Lucellan sun had been beating down upon the two of them through the dense fog that had encircled the island since the beginning of the Infection, they now found themselves cut off from all-natural light. Instead of the sun, the two were illuminated only by the flickering lights coming from a series of fluorescent lights overhead, humming and popping ominously. Ollie flipped a lever near the bottom of the stairs, flooding the entire base with artificial light.

"Hellooo!" Ollie shouted through cupped hands, the sound of his voice echoing across the base. Ben put his hand out to silence him; if any of the Infected were loose in the base, then Ollie's cry would surely bring them right to the two boys. If the man on the other end of the walkie-talkie was here, this was a rescue mission, too. Whoever that man was, he knew more about

the Infection than he had let on, and Ben had come too far now to not get to the bottom of all this.

"Check around downstairs." Ben pointed toward the hallway, gray and lined with red chairs and shelves. "Meet me back here in five minutes if you don't find anything. And be careful," Ben chided gently. Ollie nodded, disappearing into the elevator and descending to the lower level.

Ben turned on his heel, following the overhead lights throughout the ground floor. The first room he came upon seemed to be some sort of office room, nine cubicles all separated with glass walls. Ben searched through the offices for anything they could use but came up mostly empty-handed. A few half-full staplers, a couple of long-disconnected phones covered in cobwebs. If the mysterious voice on the other end of the walkie-talkie *had* come from here, it was not recently. No one had been here in a very long time.

Ben moved on to the next room—this one much smaller, empty except for a few scattered papers and abandoned test tubes. He pulled a heavy-duty flashlight out of Officer Doggy's bag, just one of several things he has saved from the veteran of the Lucella Police Department's stash when he had disappeared from the woods that night, all those weeks ago. Shining the beam from the flashlight across the papers on the table, Ben began to read, piecing together what he could from the complicated formulas and notes scrawled unevenly across the pages. He flipped through them, his eyes widening as he pieced everything together. Taking a deep breath, he suddenly became aware of how quiet it was. The hair on the back of Ben's neck stood on end as he became aware of the sound of footsteps behind him. Clutching Officer Doggy's flashlight in his grip, he whirled around to face the source of the echoing footsteps.

"Wah!" Ollie screamed when, confronted with Ben, who was poised to strike.

"Ollie, what are you doing? You can't sneak up on people like that, we are on *high alert*!"

Ollie took a moment to catch his breath. "You *just* told me to be quiet!" Ben clicked Officer Doggy's flashlight off and stowed it back in his backpack.

"What did you find downstairs?"

"Not much. Just some auxiliary power and a whole bunch of cobwebs. What do you think they were cooking up in this place?"

Ben motioned Ollie toward the notes he had found. On the front page of each was a mishmash of different handwriting, overlapping notes, and formulas. On the back of every page was a strange series of lines and circles. Ben didn't understand, but he figured that they were important. "Ollie, I think we were wrong. I don't think this is a military base, I think it's a lab. A lab designed to manufacture a cure."

Ollie's eyes widened. "A cure? For the Infection? You really think so?"

"It would explain these notes. They mention something called *Substance-128*. It sounds like whatever that is, it was the reason for the original Infection. There are some parts that I don't completely understand, something about limoncello—no, Linaeomma—"

"Ben, I hate to interrupt . . ." Ollie spoke up, but Ben

had sensed it, too. They weren't alone, and this time Ben was sure that the interloper was not a friend. The footsteps of the people infected by the virus were almost unmistakable. Though they seemed to glide when they walked, their footsteps were heavy and plodding. Glowing red eyes appeared in the doorway, on a creature taller than Ben and Ollie by a great deal, and they were getting closer by the moment. The hulkish frame of the Infected disappeared and reappeared beneath the lab's faulty lighting.

"Don't . . . move . . . a muscle," Ben whispered to Ollie through gritted teeth. The lumbering figure advanced another step, then another. Ollie took off, disappearing through the adjoining door.

Predictably, the monster took off after him, leaving Ben alone to rifle through Officer Doggy's old bag. The flashlight, some granola bars . . . Ben finally got his hands on what he had been looking for, Officer Doggy's old Taser. It was only powerful enough to stun one of the Infected for a couple of seconds, but sometimes that was all you needed. Ben shoved all the research notes into Officer Doggy's bag and slung it over his shoulders before chasing Ollie and the Infected out the door.

It didn't take long to spot his friend, weaving through the mazelike corridors of the offices—the Infected not far behind. Ben moved through the offices as well, taking care not to get too close to his target. If there was a cure out there, Ben wanted to make sure he wasn't a zombie himself when they found it. Ollie continued to run, making a break for the laboratory doors. The creature advanced on Ollie as Ben zigzagged through the office, finally exiting on the other side.

Catching up to Ollie and his pursuer, Ben stood in front of the door to the lab. He raised the Taser to his eye level and aimed it at the bear creature, steadying his shaking hands. If Ben hadn't been so focused on rescuing Ollie, he may have noticed the sounds on the other side of the door. The subtle thudding on the door had been growing less subtle by the second, and finally the door to the secret laboratory groaned loudly as it caved inward, Billy and Badgy bursting through just in the nick of time. The force of the sudden intrusion knocked Ben over as Billy barreled through the now-open door. Ben should have known that these two were not the type to figure out a four-digit pin code. Why open a door when you can make one?

Badgy ran directly into battle, forcing the Infected away from Ollie with a series of precise blows from his glowing rod. Billy stepped in and closed the door behind them, slotting his weighted barbell across the door to barricade it from any unwanted visitors. The Infected that they had stumbled across in the lab snored at Badgy's feet, seemingly unconscious. Badgy sheathed his glowing weapon on his hip, pointing to the unconscious bear.

"Tell me that wasn't the voice on the radio," Badgy said.

Ben shrugged and sighed. "That's going to have to take a back seat. Take a look at these." Ben bent over to pick up the notes from the lab, which had scattered on the ground when he had fallen over. "Wait a minute . . ." From this angle, Ben could suddenly see the markings on the back of the notes in the proper light. They weren't random sketches when they lined up like this. "It's a map!" Ben exclaimed. It was all starting to make sense. Whoever had been working at that base knew that the virus was spreading. Maybe they wouldn't have time to complete the cure, but they could leave clues for people who could.

"Umm . . . a map to what?" Billy queried. "Buried treasure? The homes of the stars?"

"A cure, we think," Ollie answered, helping Ben grab the papers. Billy and Badgy looked over the notes and handed them back to Ben, who stowed them again in Officer Doggy's bag. "I was thinking, there's nothing here but some old beam radiation machines . . . But there's gotta be almost a half-dozen locations on this map. If we all split up, and each explore one—"

"Whoa, whoa, whoa . . . back it up there." Badgy halted Ben's train of thought before he could take it to its logical conclusion. "There's four of us, and a whole lot more of them out there. No one is splitting up anywhere. If this is a map to a cure, we find it together. And if it's just a whole bunch of nonsense . . . Well, we do that together, too."

"That was . . . surprisingly wholesome of you, Badgy," Ollie commented.

"Relax, I just don't want to have to whack any of you guys with this thing." Badgy recoiled, patting the glowing rod that he kept at his hip.

"We should get going," Ben said, moving toward the door.

"Uhh . . . not that way," Billy cautioned. "We blocked it behind us for a reason." Ben understood instantly. That explained why Billy and Badgy had been in such a hurry to get inside the lab.

"How many?" he queried. Fighting off the Infected had turned into a way of life for Ben over the last couple of months, but no matter how good you got at it, it was always preferable to avoid them when you could. The virus had made the Infected impossible to reason with, extremely aggressive, and incredibly contagious. A simple swipe from one of the Infected could have you joining their ranks before the day was done. That was why this cure was so important.

"More than are in here," Badgy replied, gesturing to the sole Infected at his feet. The bear began to stir and groan as if in response, but a singular rap on the head from Badgy's glowing weapon set it right again, the creature falling back into unconsciousness. "Is there a back way out of here?" Three pairs of eyes fell on Billy, who was retrieving his weighted barbell from the door, the sounds of infected groans echoing on the other side of the makeshift entrance. Billy paused.

"Why . . . Why is everyone looking at me?"

The sound of metal and concrete crunching echoed across the base as Billy punched another hole in the other side of the lab. Badgy, Billy, Ben, and Ollie climbed through just as dozens of zombified creatures swarmed the lab, shambling around in the low light, looking for something to eat or destroy.

Billy delivered a superstrong blow to their exit, his incredible strength causing bricks to topple over, barricading the Infected inside. The quartet collapsed in the grass, taking a moment to catch their breath and regather their wits. Ben pulled a bottle of water from Officer Doggy's bag, rebolstered the Taser, and

packed it away. He retrieved the notes, this time assembling them in the form of the map.

"A cure . . . I can't believe it," Ben said softly, almost to himself. If only he had known about this earlier. Officer Doggy, Bunny . . . the people he could have saved. "So, what do you figure? You think the scientists from the lab all split up and took their part of the cure to different places? Or . . . there's a missing ingredient on the list; maybe they went to look for it?"

Badgy sat up, wiping sweat from his brow. "Yeah. Or maybe they were a bunch of knuckleheads who locked themselves underground with a bunch of zombies, and now they've all got *the ick*."

"Someone's being a bit of a *Debbie Downer* again," chided Billy gently.

"You know that's not my name!" replied Badgy sharply. "Look at these notes. See what's circled over and over? Substance-128. Do you know what that means?"

"Of course," Billy replied matter-of-factly. "It means one of the missing scientists was an Aquarius."

"*What?* No. It means whatever caused this virus, they had one hundred and twenty-seven other versions. Who knows how many times it's going to take us to make a cure. *And what did I tell you about that astrology stuff?*"

"If we do it right, Badgy . . . just once," Ben said, confidence in his voice covering the fact that the badger was right. Ben was no scientist. "If this thing is the real deal, we can help a lot of people."

"Yeah, yeah. Save yourself the rousing call to action. You've practically already convinced the big lug, and who knows where he'd end up without me. So what's the first move?" The conversation was interrupted by the sound of static. The sound startled Ben to a jump; he had forgotten he still wore the walkie-talkie clipped to his belt.

"Hello?! Hellooo?!" a garbled voice on the other end of the line cried out. Ben unclipped the device from his waist, pressed the transmission button, and spoke into the receiver.

"This is Ben, we copy you." The sound of static

again, and then silence until a distorted, heavy sigh came across the speakers.

"Oh, thank goodness. We lost contact, we were afraid . . . Where have you been?"

"Sorry, Willow," Ben apologized over the walkie-talkie. He had promised Willow that he and the rest of the crew would check in frequently with reports on their progress, but with everything that had occurred since they left The Safe Place, Ben was just now realizing that they hadn't been in contact in days, if not longer. "We must have lost signal when we went underground."

"And . . . what were . . . you doing . . . underground?" came the garbled reply. The signal aboveground wasn't much better, now that they were a sizable distance away from The Silver Paw and their safe place. The sounds of an obvious commotion in the background of Willow's call certainly didn't help.

"It's a long story, Willow," Ben responded with a light chuckle. "We'll tell you when we get back." Over the silence from the opposite end of the walkie-talkie,

Ben could just imagine that piercing glare that Willow was giving him.

"You're lucky I have to deal with . . . *whatever* the twins are doing right now, Ben. I expect *real* answers next time we speak."

"And I hope I have some for you," Ben replied. "Signing off." Ben turned the radio dial on the walkie-talkie to the off position and stashed it back in the bag.

"So . . . is anyone going to tell me why we didn't just tell Willow about the cure?" Billy finally asked, breaking the silence.

"Come on, you know how Willow is. If she finds out there is a chance there's a cure out here, she'll send in every Silver Paw agent she's got. We don't even know what these papers mean. All we have are a bunch of scattered notes on something called Substance-128, and a newspaper clipping about . . . *lemon—*"

"Linaeomma," Badgy corrected. "It's an illness. The only confirmed cases are on the island. My—" Badgy stopped himself and cleared his throat. "It's supposed to be extremely rare."

"You think that's what they were doing in that lab? Trying to create a cure to cure their last cure?" Ollie piped up.

"I think if we don't get moving, it won't matter," Badgy replied, and he was right. On the other side of the laboratory walls, Ben could hear the unmistakable agitated grunting of the Infected. Ollie grabbed a steel rebar from the pile of toppled bricks, gearing up to defend himself as he had done for so long on his own.

"Where are we headed first, Ben?" Ollie inquired, his young voice wavering slightly as he held out his makeshift weapon, prepared to jab at anything that came through the barricaded entrance. Ben flipped through the papers urgently, consulting both the notes and the map. These had clearly been written by people smarter than Ben.

"There's a lot of chemicals here that I don't recognize," Ben admitted, skimming through the first page

of notes and reading off a list of dozens of assorted compounds and solutions.

"All right, that sounds good. Let's go, then!" Ollie yelled, placing the steel bar in his belt loop in a similar way to how he had seen Badgy do the same thing dozens of times. He set off down the opposite side of the hill, Badgy and Billy in tow as the sun began to set over the horizon.

"Wait!" Ben cried as he traipsed down the hill after them. "Shouldn't we have some kind of plan? Do you even know where to get half these things?"

"Oh, Ben . . ." came Ollie's sweet reply. "How many times do I have to tell you that you should pay attention in class?"

Ø Ø Ø

By the time the foursome had made their way back into town, Ben's legs were running on borrowed energy. He had refused the hospitality of The Silver Paw at first, but knowing that he had The Safe Place to return to and that his parents were being taken care of was a load off his mind, if not his legs. Night had fallen hours ago by the time they reached the school. Ollie had been right; if Ben had paid more attention while he was in class, he would have recognized most of the chemicals listed on the notes from the lab. In Ben's defense, the last time he had stepped foot in this school, it had not been for academic reasons.

The events replayed in Ben's head like they had just happened to him yesterday. He had been looking for Ollie, and after escaping from one of the Infected, he had gone to the police station for help. The police station was already in a state of disrepair; the virus had already taken its toll there, but Ben had managed to escape with the help of Officer Doggy. Ben had outsmarted one of the zombielike Infected and filled an escape car with gasoline, allowing him and Officer Doggy to drive away from the station. They had run out of gas in the middle of the road and fled to the woods. That was the last time he had seen Officer Doggy, that night in the forest. Ben hoped the officer was all right, thriving somewhere off this virus-stricken island, but hope was all he had. On the edge of the forest, he had found the walkie-talkie that led him to the school on a rescue mission. That was how he had met Bunny, another in a long line of quick friends. Bunny had seemingly sacrificed herself at the Metro station to buy Ben enough time to get onto the train.

Ben shook his head to clear his thoughts, his fists clenching in resolve. That had been then, this was now. He was not going to lose anyone close to him this time around. He was going to save people. The quartet formed a small huddle as they reached the front door of the school. They were going to need a plan. There was no accounting for being taken by surprise, and this time they knew that they were walking into enemy territory. Just by looking up into the foggy night sky, several of the Infected could be identified by their silhouettes against the classroom windows.

"All right, the last time I was here, there were two Infected, I think. One in the math classroom and one in the chemistry lab," Ben explained to the group. "Now obviously, the chemistry lab is our goal tonight." Billy's hand slowly raised into the air. "Um, yes, Billy?"

"Were there any Infected in the social studies class-room last time you were here?"

"Uhh . . . I don't think so?"

Billy pumped his massive fist. "Social studies was always my favorite."

"Okay . . ." Ben trailed off. "Any other questions?"

"Nah," Badgy said. "Let's just get this over with. This place gives me the heebie-jeebies." Ben nodded and pushed open the front door. Badgy was right; even before this place had become a nesting ground for the Infected, it hadn't exactly been welcoming. Un-like the daylight flooding the lower levels of the lab when they had entered, artificial light spilled out as Ben pushed the door open, illuminating their faces as they entered the school. Even with a host of zom-bies using it as their home base, the building still smelled unmistakably like a school. The smell of old books, chalk dust, and *cafeteria* filled the air, undercut only slightly by the smell of zombies. Still, much of the school looked just as it always had. The hallways and conference room seemed clear, but as the front door clicked shut loudly behind them, Ben heard the stirrings of the Infected, an unmistakable grunting sound as they rose from their virus-induced slumbers.

Billy and Badgy followed Ollie and Ben, deferring to their expertise as they moved down the hallway toward the chemistry lab. Rows of deep-red lockers lined the hall, each stacked uniformly against cool-gray walls. Each step that Billy took shook the ground, causing the lockers to rattle gently. The groaning was growing louder. Down the hall, a dozen Infected poked their heads out of classrooms, eager to see what the noise was, and if it could be devoured.

"Do you remember the list of things we're here to get?" Ben asked Badgy quietly.

"Not a single one, mate," Badgy replied honestly.

"Then you have just volunteered to be a distraction." The chemistry lab was at the end of this hallway, but the six infected creatures that stood in their way didn't look as if they were partial to discussions of reason. As they advanced, their glowing red eyes focused on Billy and Badgy, who seemed to get the message almost immediately. Badgy shouted loudly—a war cry—before plowing through the middle of the group of zombies. Billy followed after, charging after Badgy, his barbell extended and his footsteps rattling the lockers noisily. In an instant, the pair had disappeared down the hallway, with the infected creatures in hot pursuit.

Following Badgy and Billy's distraction, the Infected abandoned their places in the classrooms. Making a mad dash for the chemistry lab, Ollie and Ben each took one side of the lab, tearing it apart in search of what they needed. Ollie was methodical and precise, knowing the contents of each vial and beaker that he picked up and tucked into his waistband. Ben, on the other hand, was grabbing anything and everything he saw, throwing anything that looked even remotely helpful into Officer Doggy's backpack. Ben didn't know how much of a window he could count on Badgy and Billy for. Better to grab everything and sort out what they didn't need later. A telltale clang sound gave Ben even more incentive to pick up the pace;

he would know the sound of Billy's barbell colliding with someone's head anywhere. He stuffed more test tubes, beakers, and vials into the bag, throwing a thumbs-up over his shoulder to Ollie, who returned the gesture. Ben hurriedly zipped Officer Doggy's bag shut, its contents now clinking against one another as he slung the bag over his shoulder and ran out the door.

Once again, Ollie was right when he said that Ben should pay more attention in school. Colliding almost directly with one of the Infected, Ben practically bounced off the creature's chest, the smell almost instantly overpowering him.

He rolled to avoid smashing any of the tubes in the bag. The creature was nearly twice his size. It opened its mouth to let out a bloodcurdling roar, only to be met with a sharp swat from the steel bar Ollie had taken from the lab. The thing recoiled, stunned, and Ollie swatted it a few more times until it fell to the ground, unconscious. The duo hopped over the passed-out Infected, shutting the door behind them. A red key hung from the doorknob and Ollie jammed it into the matching keyhole, twisted it and locked the infected creature in the classroom, before the two took off down the hall after their friends.

Their friends, fortunately, were not hard to find. Four of the Infected tried to force their way through one

doorway all at once, Badgy audibly antagonizing them from the other side. Ollie dispatched one of the Infected with his steel bar while Ben took down another with Officer Doggy's Taser. Stuck between

Ben and Ollie and their prey, the two remaining Infected pushed themselves through the doorway, only to be taken down by a weighted barbell and a glowing jade rod. All the Infected now were down, except for one. Lunging at Billy, the creature slashed, only to be met with a dull thud from a thick textbook. The creature recoiled, then fell as Billy tossed the textbook to the side. "Social Studies . . . always my favorite subject," he noted fondly, letting out a breath he had been holding for what seemed like forever. "Did you guys get what you needed?" Ben hoisted his bag up, stoppered test tubes clinking against one another affirmatively.

"You think we can get out of here, now?" Badgy whined. "I've had enough nightmares where I end up back in school." Ben let out a tense chuckle as he reached out a hand to pull Ollie to his feet. Navigating their way back to the front doors of the school was most certainly a less arduous task than getting to the lower classrooms. The infected creatures they had taken down in the classroom were already beginning to stir, their horrible groans echoing throughout the hallways, but the group had more than enough of a head start. Ben led the way, pushing the double doors of the school building open, and the four adventurers were greeted by the ever-present chill in the Lucellan air. The quartet took a moment to catch their breaths—it seemed that was all the time there was these days—a moment.

Their moment was interrupted by the familiar but abrupt screech of Officer Doggy's walkie-talkie. Ben scrambled to dig the device out from the old bag as Willow's authoritative bark came through as a garbled mess. The farther they got from The Safe Place, the more the signal seemed to be fading. Ben pressed his ear to the communication device, gently twisting the knob that focused the signal until he found the clearest frequency. "Come in, Willow. We hear you now."

"Well, finally! I've been trying to reach you clowns for the better part of a half an hour!" Ben extended his arm, holding out the walkie-talkie so the others could hear, though Willow was having no problems making her voice heard through the outdated device.

"Sorry, boss. We've been busy," Badgy answered into the walkie-talkie. This was clearly not the answer that Willow was looking for.

"See, this is what I'm talking about. *Underground* this, *busy* that. What are you four up to? What did I say last time we spoke?"

"That you had to see what the twins were up to?" Ollie piped up.

"I said that I wanted real answers!" Willow growled back.

Willow's tinny reply elicited no answers from anyone. Ben met the eyes of everyone in this small group individually, wordlessly weighing their options and gauging their responses. They couldn't keep Willow out of the loop forever and run around the island of Lucella as mavericks, raiding laboratories and school buildings in the hopes that they had correctly interpreted the scrawled notes of a bunch of scientists that no one had ever seen. Their other option was to tell Willow what they were doing. Perhaps she could help, but more than likely she would devote all The Safe Place's resources and people to assisting in the search for the cure—people and resources that could be better used to keep The Safe Place deserving of its name. Ben's parents were there along with half the people he had met on this journey. If telling Willow a few white lies was the price of keeping all those innocent people safe, then perhaps it was worth it. Ben met Ollie's eyes, relaying all that with a look, then nodded.

"Hello? Hello?" came Willow's voice from Ben's outstretched palm. "If you guys are doing something,

38

I would like to remind you that this is a very auditory medium!"

Ben pressed his finger to the transmit button, stammering as he spoke. "No! Uh, everything's perfectly all right now. We're fine . . . We're all fine here now. Thank you. How are you?" Ben winced, cringing at his own attempt to fly casual. It was Willow's turn to be silent for a moment.

Finally, the walkie-talkie crackled again, and Willow cleared her throat on the other end. "Is someone going to tell me what's going on?"

It was Billy who finally cracked. Ben's finger was barely on the transmitting button when Billy burst, the truth spilling from him like a broken dam. He talked about the underground military base and how it was actually an underground military lab. He told about the mysterious documents and the map that was formed when they were put together, and he told all about their adventures since they had left The Safe Place, and the ingredients they had already collected. This time both parties were silent, Billy clutching hooved hands to his mouth as if he could somehow hold back the flood of information that he had just spat out over the airwaves. As if there was anything left to hold back. After what felt like several minutes, another heavy sigh crackled over the walkie-talkie.

"You four come back to The Safe Place. This is officially a Silver Paw operation." Ben, Ollie, Badgy, and Billy all reacted loudly, but Willow shouted over their dismay. "I said this is a Silver Paw operation! I'll send a pair of agents out to each of the locations, and we'll have them bring the components back to The Safe Place. We can do any testing—"

"And how long will that take?" Ben interrupted. "With all due respect, Willow, people are getting turned into those things every day. People with families, people with people who care about them. We're not going to let you send a dozen other people out there. They've got their own families to look after. They've got *my* family to look after. We've got this. Right?"

"Right," Ollie agreed.

"Right," Billy said, nodding aggressively.

"You know, I'm gonna be honest, I'm pretty hazy on our odds," Badgy admitted, looking around at the motley crew that had apparently just tasked itself with saving the world. A powerful elbow bump from Billy sent Badgy almost off his feet. "*But* . . . but if the kid says we've got it . . ." The sound of a dull thud echoed over the walkie-talkie, almost like the sound of an ax hitting wood or an adult-sized head hitting a mahogany desk.

When Willow's voice came through the line again, she was speaking through gritted teeth. "At least tell me what the next component to the cure is." Ollie looked to Ben, who nodded, for confirmation. Ollie unzipped Officer Doggy's backpack, pulled the weathered documents out of the bag, and sorted through them. Ollie moved through the backpack taking inventory and listing for Willow everything that they had procured from the laboratory and the school's chemistry lab.

Finally, he found the piece of the map with the next ingredient of the cure scrawled hastily across it. "Well . . . This is just silly," Ollie opined, looking at the front and back of the paper, even turning it upside down to see if there was something that he was missing.

"What is it?" Ben asked, realizing that in the hurry, haste, hope, and confusion that he had neglected to sit down and really study the Cure Papers. He was no scientist, but he would have to have a pretty room-temperature IQ to lead his friends on a wild goose chase after all they had been through together.

"It's just a bunch of doodles," Ollie said, showing the page around. True to his word, there were a few chemical compounds scribbled in the margins of the page, but they had long established that no one in this quartet was much of a scientist. The rest of the page was decorated almost exclusively with doodles of bright red apples. Well, parts of apples, anyway. Top to bottom, front and back, pictures of apples that were split open to reveal their white innards and brown seeds. The group pondered their next clue for a moment.

"Well, at least we have one of the scientist's names," Billy said, resigning himself from the groupthink. He hopped up, picked up his barbell, and began to curl it as he waited for the others to conclude their brainstorming.

"What are you talking about, Billy?" Badgy questioned his old friend. Clearly the muscular bull saw something that the others didn't. Some hidden message among all the poorly drawn fruit portraits.

"It's right there in the tiny print. Amy G. Dallin."

The other three peered closely at the frayed edges of the paper, and sure enough there it was, scrawled almost imperceptibly several times across the note. Billy must have had astounding eyesight, or maybe he was just drawn to the color red. Baggy snatched the sheet from Ollie and pressed it to his face, squinting closely at it. "That don't say Amy G.—that's one word. And I don't think you can get that at a grocery store or anything."

"You know it's an absolute wonder you lot have survived this far. Don't you people know what *amygdalin* is?" Willow asked. She wasn't wrong. As the leader of The Silver Paw, Willow oversaw dozens of highly trained agents. Top of the line, these four were not. Willow gripped the walkie-talkie tighter. Her question was greeted by a chorus of *nos*, except for Badgy. "But if you want to explain it to the kids, then, by all means, be my guest."

"It's a sort of sugar, a chemical found in fruit seeds," Willow explained over the walkie-talkie. "You know, apples, cherries, peaches, watermelon, nectarines . . ."

"Yeah, we know what fruits are," Badgy grunted. He whispered as an aside: "That's why I didn't guess the fruit seed thing, by the way. It's 'cuz she didn't draw any nectarines."

Another mystery cracked. This was perfect; there was a grocery store by the Metro. They could stock up on all the fruit seeds they needed, and maybe even grab some food and supplies for themselves. Willow's voice crackled again over the walkie-talkie. "Tell me what the next component of the cure is, and I'll send some men out ahead of you," Willow said, pulling rank with only the tone of her voice.

"Oh no . . . We're going through a tunnel," Ben said flatly, turning the walkie-talkie off with a flick of his wrist and clipping it back onto the loop of his belt.

"So glad we got *that* figured out." Billy exhaled, breaking the silence.

"You are a *blabbermouth*," Ollie said pointedly, packing up the Cure Papers into Officer Doggy's bag and zipping the backpack carefully.

"Aw, leave 'im alone. In his defense, she did help us figure out the apple clue. Were any of us gonna get that? Maybe the kid, eventually, but hey. I'm no good at this chemical equation stuff. Once people start talking about molar mass, my eyes glaze over." Badgy grabbed the glowing rod from the ground and placed it back in the makeshift scabbard he wore on his hip.

"You don't think that's a little strange coming from you?" Ollie questioned as they finally pushed off from the school, leaving the silhouette of Infected in the windows of the stairwell behind them. "I mean, that's not exactly a cricket bat that you're walking around with." Badgy flipped his radioactive rod twice, caught it in hand, and then tested the balance in his palm.

"This old thing? She's got nothing to do with science. My old man's brother worked at the power plant over in Doveport. He gave this to me when I was just a little baby badger cub. He said to me, he said, 'Hold on to this, Badgy. When the time comes . . . you'll know what to do.'"

Ollie let the story sink in for a moment before he asked the question on everyone's mind: "So? Has the time come?"

Badgy let out a noncommittal grunt and shrugged while sheathing the rod back into its scabbard. "I dunno, I'd hafta say it's come in pretty handy for busting zombie butt." Again, these days, sometimes that was all that you could hope for. "So, where to next?" Lucella was a small island, but there was more than one grocery store.

Several of them littered the city, and the supermarket was the most obvious answer. Unfortunately, it was most likely a popular choice with the zombie infected population of Lucella as well. Even before the Infection had begun to spread, that place had been a madhouse. Ben was sure that it was the last place he wanted to go. Well, the last place he had wanted to go during a zombie apocalypse was the mall, but that ship had sailed a while ago.

"There's a grocery store on the Metro line," Ben announced decisively, after thinking for a long minute. Ollie nodded; he knew it well. It was the very same grocery store that Ollie had been going to since he was a younger child, on trips with his grandparents. The ground rumbled beneath their feet, and, as if in agreement with their plan, the train belowground arrived according to schedule, even during a zombie apocalypse. The island of Lucella knew the importance of stable transit in these modern times. The quartet finished gathering their things, and together traipsed down the stairs to the train station.

The feeling was familiar, but at the same time so

different. The last time he had gone from the school to the train station, he had been searching for Ollie; this time his friend was right by his side. Last time, he had only a stranger for company; this time he was surrounded by friends. Last time he had been hiding, running from creatures he knew nothing about; this time he was leading the charge. The last time he had made this journey, he had felt only dread, a knotted, gnarled pit in his stomach. This time . . . dare he admit that he felt a sense of hope? That maybe not everything that he had been through over the last

several weeks had been for nothing? Of course, some things never changed.

At the bottom of the steps, there were more of the Infected than Ben could ever remember seeing in one place. Ollie began to slowly back up the steps, drawing the steel bar he had taken from the lab. Looking around, Ben could see that Badgy's glowing staff and Billy's barbell were already drawn as well. Ben made a note to himself to get a signature weapon as he shifted Officer Doggy's backpack to his front and rifled through it, shoving the Cure Papers, the stoppered test tubes from the chemistry lab, and Officer Doggy's flashlight aside as he fumbled for the police officer's Taser. Shoving everything else back into the bag, he zipped it up and flipped it onto his back, assuming the same ready position as his friends.

PIGGY: THE CURE

The train station looked exactly the same as Ben remembered it, perhaps in a greater state of decay, if that were possible. He scanned the crowd for Bunny, not sure if he was relieved or disappointed when he didn't see a telltale pair of oversized ears sticking out from the crowd of infected people. A dull whine told Ben that his Taser was ready and he fired at the first of the Infected who advanced toward him. Like always, it only seemed to stun the giant creature for around ten seconds, but sometimes that was all you needed.

The creatures lurched toward the group, moving in the strange, gliding way that only the Infected could. The group split up, each drawing their own crowd of the infected toward them. Ollie's time on the streets of Lucella seemed to have served him well—he dipped, ducked, dove, and dodged like a professional, the glowing eyes of the Infected barely able to keep up with him, let alone their rigid legs. Badgy seemed to want to tease the Infected. Each thrust and parry of his glowing rod seemed to stun them for less than a minute, but he would use this time to his advantage, discombobulating several of the creatures at once.

And then there was Billy, whose massive strength seemed to make all these creatures little more than an annoyance to him. He casually knocked yet another of the Infected aside with his giant barbell, the creature's head lolling back as it was sent to a blissful ten-second nap.

Ben looked around the subway station, the same dull whine reminding him that he had a fully charged Taser at his disposal. He fired the machine again, an electric charge sending another one of the Infected into a seizing fit. Ben stepped over the creature, apologizing quietly as the thing snarled and growled before falling into what Ben assumed was a peaceful doze. Ben peered over his friend's shoulders again, waiting for the sound to tell him that he was safe to use Officer Doggy's Taser again. Finally, he saw what he was looking for, a pair of yellow orbs floating in the endless mass of angry red ones.

As the floating yellow beams grew closer, they illuminated the Metro station passageway, scaring some of the Infected away. The yellow high beams of the train came to a stop just in front of the group. Ben ran down the stairs, desperate to take this train out of here. Normally, Ben was fine to "catch the next one," but the stakes were a little bit higher here. The smell of an old outdoor puddle filled Ben's nostrils as he made a break for the open train doors, one of the infected creatures popping up between Ben and the air-conditioned train car meant to take him to his next destination. As if by habit, Ben gripped the handle of Officer Doggy's weapon, sweating fingers

clutching the trigger. Ben squeezed, expecting the infected boar to go down with a squeal of rage. Expecting the Taser to release a charge and buy him the ten seconds that he so desperately needed this time. Expecting anything but the dull click of a Taser that had not yet had time to recharge.

Ben cursed his luck as he threw the temporarily useless zombie deterrent back into Officer Doggy's backpack. The thing roared, making it instantly and abundantly clear that whatever these infected creatures valued, it was not dental hygiene. The boar lifted its massive arm, threatening to attack Ben when, with a thwack that resonated across the cavernous walls of the train station, it was laid out by simultaneous blows from a steel bar, a glowing rod, and a weightlifter's barbell. It was Ollie's turn to pull Ben to his feet. "Come on, man. You have to stand clear of the closing doors," Ollie said, a hint of a grin crossing his youthful face. Was Ollie quipping now? Ben would have to get him away from Badgy as soon as possible when this was all over, he noted. He leapt to his feet, joining Ollie, Badgy, and Billy on the train just as the doors whisked closed. Infected pressed their lifeless faces against the glass of the windows as it pulled away, leaving all of them as nothing but pairs of glowing eyes in the darkness.

The foursome took turns sleeping as the train made its stops around Lucella. After making sure that their car was zombie free and barricading the doors with Ollie's steel bar and Billy's barbell, they figured they might as well sleep. You never knew when you were going to be able to stop and get some rest these days, and the predictable schedule of arrivals and departures from each stop was like being rocked to sleep by your city's infrastructure. Ben didn't know how many times they had ridden the train from top to bottom before they all no longer felt exhausted; feeling rested was a luxury that Ben couldn't re-member since leaving The Safe Place. Speaking of The Safe Place, Ben considered checking in with Willow and The Silver Paw, but he knew that she would just press them for information, then send her men into danger to try to scoop the cure her-self. She had most likely been trying to reach out to them, but it worked out just fine for Ben that the walkie-talkie's signal did not penetrate underground.

When the train lurched to a halt, this time the quartet stood groggily, accepting that their arduous mission had to continue sometime. For a moment, Ben would have been content to stop there and ride the train with his friends forever. Safe. Together. But if Ben and his friends didn't find proof of a cure, then that safety and togetherness was over for hundreds of other people, all across the island of Lucella. And maybe beyond. The train station they arrived at was much less popular than the one they had come from and, as a result, had far fewer of the Infected lingering around. With a loud groaning sound, Billy unwrapped the barbell and steel rod from around the doors of the train car, tossing the rebar back to Ollie. Ollie flinched but caught the piece of metal nevertheless.

Ben looked to his friends as the train doors closed and the train whooshed away, taking their only sense of safety for the past few days with it. He waved his hands toward the ground, gesturing for them to put their weapons down, and pressed a single finger to his lips. There was more than one way to deal with the infected creatures across the island of Lucella. While it may seem more glamorous to swing a rod made out of a secret radioactive material, or make a better story to beat them up with a barbell, sometimes it was smarter to not engage them at all. Ben inhaled a deep breath (never a good idea when the Infected are involved) and began to sneak quietly past them.

Most of the infected creatures in this train station were asleep—passed out on their backs, snoring in ways that echoed across the platform and caused loose dust to cascade gently from the ceiling. The ones that were awake seemed to just barely be so, following the same walking pattern back and forth. It would certainly be a problem if the group was spotted. So all they had to do was not be spotted. Ben led the way, sneaking past the sentry. Every time the Infected would turn around, Ben would wait in a corner until he walked the other way. Repeating this process three or four times had Ben at the bottom stairs, gesturing for his friends to do the same.

Ollie was next and, if anything, he was better at it

than Ben was. He was smaller and more agile, and he seemed to know where the Infected was going to turn next, every time. It was like watching a dancer do a bizarre routine. Badgy was not quite as good, almost catching the Infected's attention more than once. "Whaddaya want from me?!" Badgy whispered through gritted teeth as he joined Ben and Ollie at the bottom of the subway station steps. "I'm no super-spy! I got this glow stick on my hip—I'm carrying the whole team on my back—cut me some slack!" Billy's attempt was valiant, but it was difficult not to see a giant muscular bull making an attempt to cross a subway platform. Before the Infected could raise the alarm, Billy took care of it, the sound of his bar-bell colliding with the Infected's head echoing across the platform.

The other three stood there stunned, though not as stunned as the infected creature who had just taken the full brunt of Billy's massive strength. The bull stood to his full height as he placed the barbell across the length of his back. They were snapped out of their stupor as the creature began to groan, its stirring no doubt going to rouse the others. They rushed up the stairs, leaving yet another group of infected people in their wake.

The grocery was, of course, right where Ben had said it would be. He knew the subway route like the back of his hand; he had taken it from his house to school every day, Ollie always in tow. The sign outside gleamed in the moonlight, advertising whatever deals had been current the last time this sign had been updated. Ben was almost surprised it was still dark, but it seemed in Lucella the sun was always down or setting, and you took your luck with which one, knowing you were guaranteed an ominous layer of rolling fog.

Ben held Officer Doggy's Taser at attention as he sneaked around the corners of the grocery store's exterior. Useless as the zombie deterrent currently was, feeling it in his grip made Ben feel just a bit better, just a bit braver—like he was Officer Doggy, fending off the frenzied carriers of the virus back at the Lucella Police Department. Of course, that had not ended well, but Ben was forcing himself not to think about that, a technique that had not worked

exceptionally often over the last couple of months.

As it turned out, it was exceedingly easy to scope out your enemy's movements when your enemies were a nearly mindless hive of zombie animals who had taken up residence in what was essentially a glass house. From outside the grocery store, the four could clearly see the infected creatures' movement as they moved throughout the store. It was hard to describe the way they moved to someone who had never seen it. Somewhere between a graceful lurch and a lumbering glide, the infected creatures who were awake shambled throughout the store, creating a labyrinth with just their presence. Their awful moaning pierced the night air, only barely contained by the building. Unlike the school, this place seemed like it would be easier to get into than out of. To escape, they'd have to get past at least three of the wandering Infected, not to mention the ones sure to be sleeping in the aisles.

Ollie pressed his face to a glass window on the side of the building, pointing excitedly at something on the other side. The others joined Ollie on the side of the grocery store, cupping their hands around their eyes as they peered through the glass to get a better look. Ollie had spotted the mother lode, a stack of apples about three feet off the ground. It had obviously been a while since this grocery store had seen fresh supply, but as long as the fruit still had viable seeds, they could grab them and be on their way to the next location on the map. It wasn't as if they were trying to bake a pie. Ben's stomach grumbled at the mere thought of pastry-based desserts; he hadn't had a proper meal since they had left The Safe Place. Willow may have been a pain in Ben's rear, but she at least made sure that her soldiers and guests stayed well fed. There was, but of course, one problem. The same issue as always, the singular problem that had been plaguing Ben since he had left Ollie's house all those nights ago. Asleep atop the pile of apples was one of the infected boars, stomach heaving with each labored breath that it took. Even through the glass, the thing was clearly snoring, its mouth open wide and a long, gooey tendril of drool snaking its way out of the thing's mouth.

Ben unzipped Officer Doggy's backpack, shoving the contents to the side compartments to make more room for the food and supplies he planned to gather from the grocery store. His mother had always made a habit of never going to the grocery store without a list. She said that the instant she left the house without a list, she knew she was going to grab more than she needed or forget something important. Ben silently promised himself that he wouldn't make those mistakes.

The automatic doors whooshed open as Ben approached them, the automatic chime that signaled the arrival of a new shopper ringing hollowly across the store. The sleeping boar seemed unbothered by the chime, though a few of the infected creatures roaming the store seemed to notice and were now focused on Ben as he entered the store. Badgy entered next, fingers already wrapped tightly around the glowing rod, its otherworldly light casting dancing shadows across the store. Ollie came next, the flickering overhead light and Badgy's staff casting a shadow larger than Ollie's own body. Both, of course, were dwarfed by Billy as he brought up the rear, hitting his head on the low-hanging lighting.

The infected creatures began lumbering toward the group, but this was far from Ben's group's first time. They stuck to the rows of the grocery, ducking and weaving away from the creatures. The group made their way across the grocery store, making sure to sweep every aisle while avoiding the shambling, infected boars at the same time. Ben looked for supplies as they moved, grabbing anything he could that seemed like it wouldn't have spoiled on the shelf. Every few aisles, Ben or one of his friends would find themselves trapped, infected creatures at either end of the aisle, but with the creatures practically herding themselves into a maze of their own making, it was hardly an issue. Just a quick bop on the head with a heavy enough object tended to stun them long enough for the group to shuffle past to the next safe area, if there was such a thing in a place like this.

"Hey, kid!" Badgy yelled, panting as he narrowly avoided a powerful swipe from one of the infected boars. "You got a plan? We can't do this all day!"

"I'm thinking!" Ben hissed back, trying his best not to wake the other infected creatures he knew were sleeping just around the corner. His eyes searched around the grocery store, looking for something—anything that could help his friends out of their present prickly predicament.

The grocery store looked to have been abandoned for quite a while. The few foods that remained on the shelves had been torn into by the boars, evidenced by the shredded bags throughout the store and the crumbs on the creatures' mouths and clothes. The grocery store was a sprawling, interlaced grid of food and household supplies, aisles marked with numbered signs displaying the contents of each row. Marking the ceiling was a series of security gates; tall, barred partitions suspended from the ceiling and operated by a system of gears, to be used in case of theft. The casing holding the red-and-green gears seemed to be intact, the gears themselves missing. "Ollie!" Ben whispered loudly over the sounds of the Infected groaning, nodding upward to the gear set.

Ollie understood instantly. He had been out on his own for a while and sets of gears like this were common in Lucella. They were often in states of disrepair, but luckily they were easily fixed and operated. Ollie broke off from the pack, searching the shelves frantically. "Badgy," hissed Ollie. "Help me find the missing gears! We're looking for one red, one green." Badgy stared blankly, placing his glowing rod back at its place on his hip.

"I'll help you look," he agreed, moving to dig through the shelves on the opposite side of the aisle. "But you should know that badgers are color blind." Ollie's mouth fell downward in a concerned frown, but he continued his search. Then he saw a glint of green behind an old bag of flour. Ollie seized it and held it to his eye, judging it against the gears set into the wall. It was a perfect match. Badgy's search was not proving to be that fruitful, and a horde of infected boars were bearing down on them, this time from either end of the aisle. Badgy drew his glowing rod, in anticipation of battle.

THOK! THOK!

Two of the boars at the far end of the aisle fell to Billy's weighted barbell, the hulking bull holding a grimy but unmistakably red gear between two hooflike fingers.

"What? Bulls are famous for seeing red." A smile crossed over Billy's bullish features as he tossed the gear to Ollie, who caught it deftly with his free hand. This was true, Ollie noted, though bulls actually had a more muted, less vivid sense of vision than humans and likely could not perceive the color red at all. Ollie took the two gears and ran, drawing the attention of the boars chasing the group throughout the grocery store. Ollie was small and fast, two advantages that the boars could not claim. Weeks or months of not having to do any work for their food had made this group of the Infected particularly lethargic; they moved at a pace that could best be described as *glacial*. Ollie shimmied himself onto the shelves, crawling across the top of the aisles to where the gears were inlaid in the wall. Placing the red and green gears into their respective slots, he waited for the security grates to drop.

Nothing. Ollie exhaled in frustration, but the longer he waited for something to happen the more infected boars seemed to gather at the foot of the shelves.

Badgy and Billy were dealing with their own boars, choosing to lead them away from Ollie, but at the other end of the aisle, Ollie could see Ben raising his arms and pumping one of them quickly in a circular motion. Ollie squinted, mimicking the cranking gesture until it clicked. Of course, what was a gear set without a little manual motion? Ollie slammed the metal rod from the military lab and shoved it into the machinery, using the leverage to get the gears spinning. They groaned in protest, months of disuse echoing through the grocery store as the gears began working in tandem. Instead of lowering the security gates from the ceiling, a panel in the wall began to open, revealing a single white key. Ollie rolled his eyes, the complicated process seemingly involving yet another step.

The creaking of the gears seemed to draw the crowd of boars back to the center of the grocery store, their groaning growing louder as they pressed in on Ollie. He shimmied down the shelf as quickly as his small frame would allow, the key just out of reach. The infected creatures lumbered down the aisle toward

him; the last time that they had seen fresh food was anyone's guess.

Ollie moved to fend them off with his steel rebar, only to look back and remember it was still wedged within the gear channel as a makeshift crank. The boars huddled around the base of the shelf, the scent of a fresh, juicy snack curling in their heaving, bristled nostrils. Their snouts twitched in the air as they grunted, each hoping to catch the scent of their prey.

At the other end of the aisle, Ben stood helpless and petrified. He had spent so long with his only goal being to find Ollie. To have him snatched away after so short a time would be cruel. He had started this journey in search of Ollie, and he intended to end it with the cure in hand, and Ollie by his side. A difficult feat if his young friend kept putting himself in danger like this. But even from his vantage point across the aisle, he could tell that his longtime friend had something clever in store.

Using his steel bar, Ollie hung from one hand, dangling just out of reach of the volatile infected boars. They swiped at his dangling feet, but he expertly evaded each attempt, carefully gripping the bar as he reached his free hand down and expertly swiped the key from its stowing place. He popped the white key between his teeth, using both hands to grip the steel rebar and pull himself back onto the shelves, much to the disappointment of nearly a dozen infected boars.

Ollie took a moment to catch his breath, rolled onto his back, and spit out the key, wiping his tongue on his shirt. One of the most important things to retain during any sort of end-of-the-world scenario was a sense of hygiene. Wiping sweat from his brow, Ollie righted himself, lined up the security key with the lock, and inserted it, jostling the piece of stark white metal until it unlocked with a satisfying click.

There was no real time to relax, though. As soon as the locks gave way, the security partitions began to descend from the ceiling. At first it was a creaking, out-of-practice groan, a sound that became more and more familiar these days. Then an ominous rattling as the metal doors began to lower from the ceiling. Billy and Badgy appeared alongside Ben, the zombies they had been tasked with luring long since having abandoned the chase to investigate the noises that Ollie was causing.

Ollie leapt back to his feet, reached up, and pulled the steel rebar from the laboratory out of the headset in the wall. It took some doing, with Ollie leaning back and using his feet as leverage as he pushed off against the wall, but eventually the machinery gave way, groaning in protest. As the machinery began to whir and spin out of control—no longer held stable by the steel bar—the green and red gears clattered to the ground, rolling beneath one of the aisle shelves with a soft clattering sound. Ollie pulled the white key from the security panel, silently hoping that if anyone else came upon this grocery store looking for supplies, they weren't particularly observant.

Ollie leapt into action, dashing across the top of the shelves as the gates came rolling down. Ben tried to rush toward his old friend but was held back by his new ones. They were right, there was no use putting himself in danger as well. It turned out that Ben had nothing to worry about because Ollie leapt deftly from shelf top to shelf top as the security grates came crashing down behind him. The boars tried to follow Ollie as he made his exit, but with the gates now between them and the young boy, they were trapped. The boars pressed against the gates, and for a moment it seemed they had the numbers to overwhelm the steel-frame gates. But the more time passed, the less the boars seemed interested. It took only a few moments for the boars to resume their normal behavior. Some wandered back and forth in their newfound cage; others simply sat down and went to sleep.

Ben rushed forward, Billy and Badgy not far behind him. He held out his hand to help Ollie as he scampered down from atop the grocery store shelves, landing lightly on his feet. "Clean up on aisle three," Ollie cracked, brandishing the security key. Of the scores of infected boars, a few attempted to rattle the gate, but without the key, their efforts were in vain. Badgy clapped Ollie on the back, offering him congratulations for a job well done. Billy tested the integrity of the steel security panels, prodding them with his weighted barbell. When this seemed to be drawing the boars' attention back to the quartet, Billy quickly dropped his inspections, hustling to catch up with the rest of the group.

They had come here for a reason, and that reason was not to liberate this singular grocery store from its scourge of Infected. As they left the trapped boars behind in the frozen meat section, the quartet headed toward the front of the grocery. Without the echoing grunts of a dozen-and-a-half zombies, the grocery store felt much more like its old self. Ben guided them toward their goal, marked by a hanging sign that read FRESH FRUITS AND VEGGIES! YUM! in faux scrawled font. Ben had to stifle a derisive snort. The store may have been offering fruits and vegetables, but at this point they were long past fresh.

Maybe that would account for the smell, the odor of rotting food lingering heavily in the air. More likely, however, the source of the smell was the portly boar currently lying on his back, snoring in the middle of the fruit section. Beneath the creature's massive body lay a display of apples; the drawing was advertising the apple display and looked almost exactly like the drawing on the cure notes from the military lab.

The four ragtag adventurers froze, eight eyes locked on the hulking creature before them. Badgy's eyes widened frantically, the face of a badger whose plans were falling apart before his very eyes. Ben shrugged, an exaggerated gesture to make up for his necessary silence. When he had begun this journey, his only goal had been to find his friend. He had never wanted to become a zombie slayer or the bearer of civilization's greatest hope. Ben wasn't the kind of kid who had a plan, and if he was, he certainly hadn't factored in the appearance of a several hundred–pound zombie taking a siesta on the one thing that they needed.

Each intake of breath was an effort when the air was this thick with the breath of the infected creatures, which meant holding your breath was a near superhuman feat. Still, as the foursome searched the fresh produce section for some other fruit, *any other fruit*, they each found themselves holding their breaths. Maybe it was the exhaustion from fending off a score of other infected creatures—maybe it was the feeling hanging over their heads that if they let themselves catch their breath, they'd wake the last infected creature. Each of them scrounged around for several minutes before coming to the conclusion they had known to be true all along. Most of the "fresh fruit and veggies" in this section had gone bad long ago. If they didn't manage to loot several healthy apples from the pile beneath the sleeping boar, this entire trip would have been for nothing.

As if on cue, the sleeping boar took a deep inhalation of breath, rolling over to its side. Its stomach spilled out of the ragged red shirt it wore, and a plain red apple spilled out of the pile and onto the floor, rolling to a stop at Ben's feet. He picked it up and examined it, the timing almost too good to be true. But here it was, in his hands! A round, red apple, the reflection of the grocery store's fluorescent lighting gleaming off its ruby skin. More important, as the boar continued to contort and stretch in his sleep, he offered the promise of more apples.

Ben tossed the apple into the air and caught it, before stowing the shiny red fruit in a plastic bag that he produced from Officer Doggy's backpack. Badgy and Billy pressed forward cautiously, tiptoeing tentatively toward the sleeping *Sus scrofa*. If the creature noticed their presence, it did not react in the slightest, with the outside possibility of the occasional twitch of the ear or a loud, throat-clearing snore. Every few minutes, the creature would snore loudly through porcine nostrils, then roll over onto its back or stomach. Each time, the movement would shift the tower of apples that the creature slept on, rolling a single apple toward the group. Two or three apples was fine for baking a strudel, but if the cure required the seeds of an apple to work, they were going to need quite a few more.

The four advanced toward the sleeping creature, boxing him in from all angles. Billy drew his huge barbell from his back, ready to knock the creature out, should it wake up. Somehow, that did not seem to be an issue. As Billy held the creature at barbell-point, the other three carefully picked their bounty from beneath his sleeping form. Careful to avoid the creature's rolling, the boys filled up the plastic bag slowly but surely, red apples nearly spilling out and over the brim. Ollie reached for another apple, his hand sinking into one as he gripped it. *Rotten.* Ollie discarded the spoiled apple with a frown, wiping the sour juices on the back of his trousers. The next apple that Ben grabbed crumbled in his hands. He, too, had seemingly reached the end of the viable fruits. But that did not matter, they had gotten what they had come here for. Ben spun the bag into a twist, then knotted the handles, throwing the bag over his shoulder.

Ben let out a sigh of relief, followed by a light laugh. Part of him couldn't believe that they had done it, that they had successfully taken on the grocery store and were now one step closer to a cure. One step closer to normalcy, to setting everything right. Ben raised a single finger to his lips, the universal symbol for silence, then pointed urgently to the front entrance of the grocery store. They could make a quick exit from there, then find a place to check the map and wait it out until morning. The four deserved some rest.

They backed away slowly, each keeping their eyes fixed on the sleeping boar in front of them. Ben was especially careful, sweat beading down his brow as he took several careful, measured steps backward. He and his friends snuck past the creature toward the front door. The automatic door whisked open, the cool early morning air kissing Ben's face. He took deeper and deeper gulps of the early morning air. He didn't realize how much he had missed fresh air.

A loud clattering sound drew his attention back inside the grocery store. A red streak smeared across the white tile floor and Billy was on his back, his barbell rolling across the floor—it wasn't hard to figure out what must have happened. In his attempts to sneak backward out of the grocery, it seemed as though Billy had stepped on one of the rotting apples discarded by Ollie and slipped, dropping his main zombie deterrent in the process. The barbell kept rolling, coming to an eventual stop at the bottom of the heap of apples.

With a slight tap, the structure collapsed, the sleeping boar suddenly startled to alertness. The infected creature's red eyes shot open as confused as anyone being suddenly awoken from a nap.

"Run!" Ben cried out, waving his friends to the exit. Ollie and Badgy broke into a sprint, making their way toward the exit. Billy scrambled, clearly unwilling to leave his beloved weight behind. Stopping short of the exit, Ollie pulled the white key from his pocket and shoved it into the security panel by the door. His palms were sweaty, making the key hard to grip, but after a few minutes, the mechanism

gave way, dropping another security gate from the ceiling. The metal gate clanged around the confused creature, who roared loudly for a moment before turning around and promptly resuming his nap.

"We should get out of here," Ollie cautioned. "We can work only one security gate at a time . . ." Ollie trailed off, but Ben knew what he meant—by trapping the sleeping Infected, they had let out the horde of other zombified creatures. Their suspicions were confirmed when the sound of growling began to echo throughout the store. Billy grabbed his barbell, strapped it to his back, and ran toward the exit.

Badgy was not far behind him, and Ollie brought up the rear, opting to leave the key behind. It was of no further use to them now. Badgy, Ollie, and Billy fled the grocery store, but the automatic doors did not whisk shut behind them. Ben stood in the doorway, eyes transfixed on something in the middle distance. Just in front of the army of zombies barreling down on Ben was a tattered pack of cardboard and plastic, and inside . . . batteries.

Ben fixated on the pack of batteries, his mind on only one thing—the Taser stuffed into Officer Doggy's backpack, its charge long since depleted. Ben's fingers reached out reflexively as if the plastic zombie deterrent were already in his hands. He didn't have Billy's raw strength, Ollie's quickness, or Badgy's underhanded cunning. Without a weapon to fend off the virus ridden creatures, Ben was worse than useless. He was a liability.

Ben licked his lips, feeling his tongue stick to his upper row of teeth. Dehydration had set in long ago yet was also somehow the furthest thing from Ben's mind. The incessant growling from the Infected in the grocery section grew louder as Ben stared at the batteries, frozen in place with the paralyzing weight of indecision. Still, the longer he waited, the closer the infected animals grew to gaining on them. Ben pushed unsure feet to tile, booking it across the grocery store to the singular pack of batteries displayed on the shelf.

The relief that Ben felt wrapping his fingers around the cardboard packing fell away almost immediately as the infected animals rounded the corner—rabid, hungry, and probably none too pleased at having been locked up in a cage. Ben shoved the batteries into his jacket pocket before turning to run. The infected animals gave chase, swiping at Ben as they followed. Luckily for Ben, teamwork was not the infected creatures' strong suit. Most of the virus-afflicted boars could not stop tripping over one another. Of those that could, several had come to be distracted by the conveyor belt, on which they could shamble forever and not go anywhere.

Half a dozen of the infected boars still bore down on Ben, but he managed to duck away from them all, each coming closer than the last. He was almost to the doors, freedom just within his grasp. Another loud roar startled Ben as he ran; one of the creatures was coming at him from across the aisle. Instinctively, Ben swung the only object available to him, the plastic bag full of apples. The creature moved its massive arm at the same time, swinging at Ben with an oversized claw. The two objects met in midair, colliding in accordance with the laws of physics. The creature's clawed hand proved victorious, swiping through the plastic bag like a warm knife through soft butter.

Ben's face fell, but it was too late. As the bag tore open, dozens of apples crashed to the floor—bouncing, spilling, and rolling across the tile and throughout the store. The apples that didn't split on contact with the ground suffered a much worse fate, immediately beset upon by hungry Infected. Jowls

and teeth flashing in the early morning sun as the Infected descended upon the apples—the juicy, tart, red fruits—the closest thing to a fresh meal that they had seen in a long while. They fed like they were ravenous, too, feasting on the skin down to the core and then popping even that into their mouths. Part of Ben envied the creatures for their meal, but he couldn't remember a time he had felt so crestfallen, so hopeless.

Juice dripped down the creatures' chins as they turned toward Ben, the second-most appetizing morsel they had been exposed to in recent memory. Ben didn't even notice Billy and Badgy had pulled him back by the collar of his jacket, his hand still outstretched toward the puddle of bubbling juice where their only hope for the cure had been just moments before.

The cool, early morning air and the shock of fresh wind on his face was enough to shake Ben from his despair. Suddenly he was outside and being chased by the Infected—at least the ones who had somehow figured out the automatic door. Still, any of the creatures that managed to get out became infinitely more dangerous. The only good thing about infected creatures, if there was such a thing, was that they often became simple and easy to outsmart. Even in a group, they were driven more by hunger and impulse than anything else. This made them easy to herd, thus easy to avoid. One would think that being in an enclosed space was the worst place to be with one of the Infected. That was a common misconception—in an enclosed space, you could keep your eyes on them.

The sun peeked over the horizon as the quartet ran over the dew-soaked grass. Light had not fully settled over the island; all Ben could see as he looked back was the bobbing orbs of the Infected's crimson eyes. He turned his head and faced forward, the sight of what was ahead infinitely better than the visual of dozens of eyes bobbing over the hill.

The infected creatures' growls echoed across the skyline, a din of oinking and loud grunts. It was a sound that Ben could go the rest of his life without hearing and be perfectly satisfied. If Ben had only had time to open that package of batteries and load them into Officer Doggy's Taser, he was sure this would be playing out differently. Even the most experienced zombie survivor couldn't take on this many of the Infected, and his crew seemed to be prioritizing escape over encounter, and Ben couldn't blame them. They had seen so much in the past few weeks, and that was just since they had joined up. Badgy and Billy had been working for The Silver Paw for longer than that, combing the island for survivors and shepherding them to The Safe Place. Ben had only just barely begun to hear about all Oliver's adventures on his own, but he knew that his friend had quite a whirlwind tale of his own.

Ben pumped his legs faster, trying to think of the last time that he had forced himself to move this quickly, trying to think of anything but the sounds of impending doom receding into the background. He didn't know how long they ran; all that he knew was that they didn't stop. Not until Ben's lungs burned, not until they had left behind the neon and brick of the city and traded it for massive trees and a dirt trail. Not until the only sound left was crickets chirping in the night air. The sun had come and gone hours ago, responsible for the thick layer of sweat that complemented the grime and dirt on each of their faces.

Ben's legs gave out beneath him as he collapsed against the base of a tree. He swallowed deep lungfuls of air, taking it all in. And then he let it out. Deep, bellowing wails rumbled from Ben's chest as he began to cry. He cried for all the people that they would no longer be able to cure. He cried for Sally and for Officer Doggy, but mainly he cried for himself. He contained a sniffle when he managed to get his breathing under control, wiping bleary eyes on the sleeves of his jacket. It wouldn't do for them to see their de facto leader on the ground in a puddle of his own tears.

When his vision finally cleared, none of the other three seemed to be looking at him any differently. If anything,

they seemed to be smiling, Badgy doubled over in knee-slapping laughter. "Wh-what's so funny?" Ben asked, composing himself as quickly as he could. Billy burst into laughter as well, and it was only a matter of time before Ollie couldn't help but follow suit. They all fell to their knees, then collapsed to the ground, tears welling in their eyes as they laughed.

It was Billy who forced himself to his feet first, stumbling over himself to the tree where Ben lay resting.

He pounded on the trunk of the tree, his considerable strength causing the tree to quake to its roots. Leaves cascaded down in the wake, along with a dozen round objects, several of them hitting Ben on the head on their way down. As they bounced off Ben's head and sprawled across the patchwork of grass in front of him, Ben grabbed one and held it to his face, eyes widening.

"Apples?" Ben said in disbelief, voice barely above a whisper. The others had finally regained their composure enough to confirm.

"What else, Einstein?" Badgy teased.

"Newton," Ollie interjected.

They gestured all around them, and as Ben took it all in, he couldn't believe his eyes. As far as the eye could see, row after row of apple trees, each bearing at least two dozen of the round, tart fruits. Red, green, yellow, from Granny Smith to Golden Delicious. The same forest that had protected him all those months ago, after he had fled the police station with Officer Doggy, had come through for him again. Ben had no idea why, but for some reason, the Infected never wandered too deep into the forest.

To say that they feasted that evening would be an understatement. Billy delivered several other resounding blows to the trunks of nearby trees, each of them flush with their own version of the ripe, red fruit. The quartet stuffed their faces, not remembering the last time they had enjoyed a proper meal. With the supplies that Ben had managed to liberate from the grocery store, they managed to make and subsequently devour several meals between the four of them. Ben opened Officer Doggy's backpack, rummaging around for a spare beaker from the chemistry lab. As good as it was to have food in their stomachs, their discovery of fruit in the forest meant just one thing: that the search for the cure was still on.

Ben pulled an empty beaker from the bag, and Officer Doggy's Taser clattered to the dirt on the ground. Caught up in the height of his emotions over the last few hours, he had almost forgotten about the small device. Ben picked it up, brushed the loose dirt off it, and reached into his pants pocket to fish out the packet of batteries from the grocery store. Using his teeth to tear open the packaging, Ben took the fresh batteries in his hand as he popped the Taser open and swapped the new batteries for the old. He replaced the cover and stowed the old batteries and cardboard packaging in his jacket, to be disposed of properly later.

Ben clicked the plastic cover back into place, powering up Officer Doggy's Taser. The machine whirred to life with a high-pitched trill, electricity flowing through the handheld device. Thoroughly satisfied with the new power source, he powered it down. The significance of that bag, that Taser, this forest was not lost on Ben. The first two had belonged to Officer Doggy and all three had saved his life. At this point, multiple times over. This forest had been the last place he had seen the canine officer. Wherever he was, he hoped that he was doing well.

Ben tucked the fully charged Taser back in the bag, finally pulling out the lab beakers he had come for. Collecting the seeds from this evening's ventures, he stoppered them and tossed them back into the bag with the rest of the components of the cure. Ben pulled out the documents from the military lab, spreading them out in the proper order to form the map.

PIGGY.

The wrinkled notes made little sense to Ben. Dozens of drawings of glowing blue mushrooms littered the page, the scientific nomenclature scrawled across the margin. There were notes for the preparation of the ingredient, but nothing on where to find it, and Ben doubted they would run into another forest floor covered in exactly what they happened to need.

It was Badgy's knowledge that came in handy this time, his eyes barely scanning the page before coming up with an answer. "Oh, yeah, I know these things," Badgy stated matter-of-factly, tapping his finger to his temple to emphasize his point. "These are those weird, glowy shrooms. Problem is, they only grow at the temple in Doveport." Badgy was met with silence, Ollie and Ben staring at him blankly.

"Oh, come on. Don't tell me you all have never been to Doveport? Our sister city across the sea?"

"People don't say that," Billy piped up.

"It'll catch on," Badgy shot back.

Ben thought about it, and he supposed that Badgy had to be right. He had never considered what life outside of Lucella might look like, but it seemed that life outside of Lucella was coming to him.

"So, how do we get there?" Ollie queried, chomping loudly on another apple.

"The docks at the bottom of the island. There's tons of boats with owners who aren't coming back. I'm sure they won't mind if we borrow one," said Badgy.

Then it was settled. Tomorrow they would shove off for Doveport, and one way or another, Ben would be the farthest from home that he had ever been. The thought caused a lump to form in his throat as he looked back to how scared and inexperienced he had felt last time he had spent the night in this forest. He thought back on all that had happened since then—the battles he had fought and won, the friends he had made and lost. Ben began to make room in Officer Doggy's bag for some extra apples for their trip, but soon he succumbed to the cool, crisp air and the sweet beckoning of sleep.

The usual layer of fog crept through the trees, the sun shining through the leaves catching the young adventurers in the eyes and rousing them from their well-earned rest. They had a long trek ahead of them to the docks, but what else had the last few weeks been but one long trek? One more wouldn't hurt them. Unless it did, which was always a terrifyingly real possibility. Still, their journey was mostly undisturbed. Victims of the virus tended to shy away from direct sunlight, preferring to hide in the dark. Every now and then, they would hear the characteristic growling of a group of the Infected, causing them to adjust their route. Between the four of them, they felt there was very little that could surprise them anymore. How wrong they were.

They arrived at the docks off the Port of Lucella as the sun began to set, the light reflecting off the water as it lowered itself beyond the horizon. As usual when it came to things of a shady nature, Badgy had been correct. Most of the boats in front of them, each floating lazily in the early morning breeze, had been abandoned. It turned out that there was a dramatic downturn of interest in nautical leisure during a zombie apocalypse.

They split up, each taking a different section of the dock to explore their options. When Billy returned

with an option for the biggest boat in the harbor, Ollie countered with an offer for the one that looked the coolest. Badgy shot down both choices, pointing emphatically to a boat that he claimed had "so many secret compartments." Ben thought for a moment, pacing the dock with his thumb and forefinger on his chin. He examined all their options and was inspecting the sail of a close by boat when they heard it.

The grunting sound was always the same, no matter what the person looked like. A pair of glowing red eyes emerged from the lower deck of the boat as Ben scrambled to get back onto the docks. Ben ran, leaping from the deck of the boat to the wooden paneling of the dock and taking off toward the other end, his friends not far behind. The infected moose roared, nostrils flaring and horns pointing straight in the air as the quartet piled into a boat and began to push off. Billy lifted the anchor from the harbor floor with one swift hoisting motion and tossed the chain and heavy metal into the back of the boat without so much as a grunt of exertion. Ollie hoisted the sail, the wind tickling the white cloth but refusing to take them away.

Ben looked back at the moose, who was now off the ship and shambling down the dock toward them.

Badgy grabbed the glowing isotope from his hip, preparing for battle. "Uh . . . we gotta go, guys!" he cried out. "You think that I control wind?!" Ollie hissed back. They went back and forth, bickering loudly as the infected creature made its way down the boardwalk to them. Billy reached over the side of the boat, giving them a solid push and sending them into the sea. The moose grunted at them from the end of the dock but soon retreated back to its home, and the harbor became a small dot as the quarter sailed farther and farther toward Doveport.

It was days that felt like hours—or maybe it was hours that felt like days. Ben was finding it hard to keep track of time anymore. Every day was an end-less cycle of packing up and moving, eating where you could, and fighting off hordes of deadly zom-bie creatures. It sounded much more exciting than it actually was. The weather had finally decided to cooperate with them, a strong breeze filling the sail with wind and dragging them quickly to Doveport.

It was bizarre to be whisked away to a place that you had never been, that you had never known existed until very recently. Of course, bizarre was par for the course these days. Ben hung his hand over the side of the boat, letting his fingers skim across the water. He had never been to the sea before, and here he was crossing it. A handful of people on a leaky boat to save the world.

This time it was Badgy's voice that shook him from his rumination. "Land ho!" Badgy called, shielding his multicolored eyes from the sun. Ben and Ollie stood and scrambled to the front of the vessel to get their first look at Doveport. The pair of old friends gasped, their breath immediately turning to steam and then rising into the air. Ben made a mental note to never complain about Lucella's fog again. Snow fell across Doveport in a flurry, wind picking up flakes of the frozen crystals and whipping them around. The others looked to Ben for his lead. They had come too far to turn back now. Ben gathered his coat around him and climbed the ladder onto the docks. After Billy dropped the anchor overboard, the rest of the crew followed suit.

Badgy led the way, seemingly the only member of the group who had actually been to Doveport before. They trudged forward, Ollie wearing Officer Doggy's old uniform jacket, Badgy bracing himself with his fur, and Billy seemingly content to keep himself warm with only the power of his gigantic muscles.

They passed another school and another grocery. Life in Doveport didn't seem too dissimilar from life in Lucella. It was a shame, yet no wonder, that they had succumbed to the same thing.

"Well? There she is!" Badgy stated, throwing his arms open wide to present the temple. Badgy had not led them astray. At the top of a small mountain sat a cozy-looking stone temple, dense patches of snow capping the outer peaks.

It was an arduous trek to the top of the mountain, wind and snow whipping at their faces the whole time. They finally reached the face of the mountain, Ben's expression falling as the front of the temple was revealed. The stone structure itself was gorgeously made, stone laid atop stone with a series of caverns etched into the face of the mountain itself. In front of the entrance sat a massive boulder, and behind it? Ben didn't know. All he could hear was a deep rhythmic swooshing sound and the howling of the wind. Even with three other people helping him, Ben was not sure that he could roll that boulder away, especially in weather like this. But it seemed that Ollie was already onto a solution for their problem.

A gearbox glinted from a small, chiseled inset of the mountain, so small that Ben was astounded that Ollie had managed to spot it. Ollie grabbed his steel rebar and jammed it into the gears, bracing himself against the snowy stone floor and pushing. With a groan, the stone began to roll to the side, each turn of the gears causing the massive boulder to roll a little farther out of the way until it fell to the side with an enormous thud. Ollie retrieved and stowed his rebar, taking a quick and well-deserved bow.

The inside of the temple was lit by torches, flickering flames sending shadows dancing across the cavernous interior and immediately illuminating the source of the mysterious sound. A single, giant bladed ax hung suspended from a pendulum, swinging back and forth across a bridge's chasm. Each menacing swing of the blade parted the air with a loud swooshing sound. It seemed that this was the only way forward. Ben turned to Badgy, incredulity bubbling over on his face. "How could you forget to mention the giant chasm of death?" Ben asked over

the sound of wind rushing in from the outside.

"Don't blame me, I didn't know that was gonna be here!" Three pairs of eyes fell on him, then rolled. "It's been a while since I was last here . . ." the badger added lamely.

"Well, come on. What are you waiting for?" Ollie asked from the other side of the chasm.

The other three looked up in surprise. "How did you do that?" Billy asked, a brow quirked high on his face.

"You just have to time it right." Ollie shrugged. There had to be more to it than that, Ben figured. Though maybe there was something to it, Ben thought as Billy also made the jump across the chasm with far more finesse than the average bull his size with a barbell strapped to his back. It took several false starts, but Badgy also made it across the chasm, a few loose hairs floating lazily into the bottomless pit as the swinging ax nicked his tail.

Ben bounced up and down on the balls of his feet nervously, trying to anticipate the timing of the giant swinging blade. There was a little more at risk than a few hairs if he missed. On the other side of the chasm, he could hear his friends encouraging him and offering wildly conflicting advice. He shut them off, listening only to the loud swooshing of the blade as it swung back and forth in front of him. SWOOSH. SWOOSH. SWOOSH. Ben closed his eyes, syncing his breathing with the swinging of the ax. With eyes open only as much as necessary, Ben made the leap, the ax just missing him by a margin. He felt the blade catch Officer Doggy's backpack, knocking him off-balance as he leapt. Three pairs of hands reached out, catching Ben and pulling him up onto the thin portion of bridge that crossed the chasm. Ben wiped a layer of sweat from his brow. "What did I say? You just have to time it right," Ollie reminded. Ben nodded, helping himself to his feet.

The foursome proceeded through the inside of the temple, Badgy taking careful measured steps. "Be careful, everyone. This place could be full of traps."

"Worse than a giant swinging ax?" Ben was skeptical but nevertheless began to mimic Badgy's cautious movements. "That's kid stuff. I'm talking spikes, saw blades, maybe a pit of snakes. Real republic serial stuff."

"I don't know what that is," Ollie said, hopping from stone to stone and beginning to copy Badgy's movements as well.

"Come on, kid. You gotta work with me," Badgy complained.

A cool breeze wafted through the cavern as they moved deeper. Badgy stopped, extending the glowing rod across the group, barring them from going any farther. "What's—?" Billy's question was interrupted by the arrival of several spikes erupting from their stowed place underneath the flooring.

"A breeze." Badgy lowered his radioactive rod and shimmied past the spike trap. "Never trust a breeze underground," the badger stated matter-of-factly.

"How did they get the zoning permits for this?!" Billy asked incredulously. "And who is this a temple for?" Ollie followed up.

"Ah, am I supposed to keep track of who they're building temples for these days?" Badgy waved his hand. A series of lit torches continued to illuminate their path as they made their way through the winding caverns of the Doveport Temple.

They were lucky. Following Badgy's movements, they managed to not set off any additional traps, the cunning badger sidestepping buzz saws and spikes appearing from the ground and falling from the ceiling. Ben realized that these traps had been set in place ages ago, but it really did seem as if someone desperately did not want them to get to the center of the temple.

"Hey, Badgy," piped up Ollie's tiny voice from the back of the group. "Who's Spidella?" Badgy forged on ahead, waving the question off.

"Man, you're an inquisitive one today. I dunno, kid. Where'd you hear that?" Ollie stopped, pointing to the side of the cavernous tunnel they walked through.

"It's written all over the walls here. Look, 'Beware Spidella.'" The group stopped, all pulling to the side to investigate Ollie's claim. Sure enough, the bones of some poor fool lay in a structured heap on the ground, the words BEWARE SPIDELLA carved into the wall next to the skeleton.

The group recoiled from the gruesome display, and Badgy moved them each along quickly. "All right, nothin' to see here," the badger said, ushering them farther into the underground cavern. "Skeletons rarely warn you about good things. You've never seen a pile of bones directing you to a yard sale."

In any other situation, Ben would have wanted to stop and explore. This was his first time out of Lucella, and he had already seen so much. Giant swinging ax rooms? Underground cave tunnels? Ben was sure that they didn't have those back home. Now, with only two more items left on their cure checklist, was not the time. They moved deeper into the caverns below the temple. Down here, everything was carved from stone, illuminated only by the flickering lights from the torches that lined the side of the cave. Every few yards, a series of mysterious symbols would appear—a circle with a black dot in the middle, or a line bent at an odd angle. Cobwebs covered the caverns at every angle; it was becoming clearer and clearer that no one had been down here for a long time. At least that meant that they weren't going to run into any Infected. But then . . . who was lighting the torches?

"Aw, come on!" Badgy whined from the front of the group. It seemed they had reached their destination.

The long, winding path from the top of the mountain ended here at a large wooden door with a blue glow coming from beneath. That must have been where they kept the mushrooms. Ben stepped forward, prepared to open the door, but found no handle. He pushed as hard as he could, bracing himself against the stone floor, still to no avail.

"Ollie, you wanna give me a hand?" Ben queried, now turning around and pushing at the stone slab with his back. No help came. "Ollie?" Ben relaxed his efforts, realizing their futility almost immediately. Ollie, on the other hand, was currently transfixed with a large circular contraption off to the side of the door.

"It's a wheel puzzle," Ollie explained. "We learned about them in school. You have to line up the symbols correctly, but I don't see any sort of guide . . ." Ben looked the device over as Ollie inspected it. He didn't see a guide, but he had seen those symbols before.

"Yeah, that's the umm . . . the filled-in circle, and that's the bent, *L*-looking thing." Ollie shot Ben a curious look. "What? They're plastered all over the walls down here." Ollie looked to the wheel puzzle, then to Ben.

"Can you show me?" Ollie began to move the wheel, lining the symbols according to Ben's description.

"Uhh . . . about how long you think that's gonna take y'all?" Badgy questioned, hesitance clear in his voice. Ollie looked over the wheel puzzle again, noting how many symbols there were to match.

"About five minutes, it looks like. Why?"

"Well, you know. If you could hurry it up, I think we'd all appreciate it." Badgy spoke slowly as if his attention was elsewhere, but they were working as fast as they could. Everyone here knew what was at stake. Ben turned from the puzzle to let Badgy know as much, but the badger's attention was not on Ollie, Ben, or the puzzle. Following Badgy's gaze toward the ceiling, everything suddenly clicked into place for Ben.

Draped across every inch of the ceiling was a lattice-work of webbing, just like the cobwebs the quartet had been navigating around since they arrived at the temple. Wrapped up in the webbing were dozens of infected creatures suspended and unmoving. Ben supposed that answered the question of where everyone had gone. A glint of something in the torchlight caught his eye, light reflecting off a single thread of silk. Ben's eyes followed the thread to its point of origin on the ceiling, horrified by what he found attached.

That was no line of silk; it was a thread of webbing. Suspended from the ceiling was the largest spider that Ben had ever seen. Each of its eight legs was at least the size of Ollie, if not bigger. She dropped down her web line toward the four adventurers, fangs the size of Ben's forearm peeled back past gray lips. The creature wore a black coat over a red dress, each beset with an almost unsettling number of mysterious purple stains. As if they needed more reasons to stay away, all four of the creature's eyes glowed the same familiar red they had come to know meant Infection. Ben suddenly understood Badgy's push for urgency. "Is that Spidella?" Ben asked.

"I don't know, we didn't exchange pleasantries!" Badgy shot back.

"I just need one more symbol" Ollie cried out, his voice echoing across the cavernous underground. Ben looked over the wheel puzzle. He remembered seeing the symbols on their way down, but with the giant creature descending upon them, he was finding it hard to think of anything other than how he might become her next meal. Ben racked his brain. Plus sign, circle, square . . . What was the last one? The spider on the ceiling grew ever closer. Surrounded by stone on every side, Badgy and Billy had nowhere to run; it seemed the only way out was through. Turning the way they had come, Ben ran back toward the entrance, scanning the walls for the final symbol. He barreled past the plus sign; he knew Ollie had already finished that section of the wheel. The circles were next—two black, one white.

Ben turned a corner, a white diamond on black lines carved into the wall of the cave. A diamond that was the missing symbol. He turned on his heel to run back to Ollie, but he would have no such luck. Spidella stood in his path, six of her legs skittering across the stone floor, the other two raised as weapons. Ben opened his mouth to scream, but it was too late. The spider jabbed him with one of her arms, a searing pain accompanying the gash across his stomach. Ben fell to the ground, his head starting to swim and his temperature beginning to raise. Through his bleary vision, he could see Spidella poised to strike again. He raised Officer Doggy's

Taser and fired it, missing completely. His vision was too blurry, his arms too heavy. The last thing he saw was Billy and Badgy rushing up the path to him. But as his consciousness faded, he knew that they would be too late.

When Ben woke up, the first thing he noticed was the brightness. Underground, everything had been so dark and dank, but here . . . where was here? Ben looked around, the setting familiar to him. A wooden floor, books scattered across the floor. Across the room, a chalkboard dusted with the imprint of the eraser.

"Hang on, I'm feeling a little off . . ." Ben said to no one in particular as he pinched the bridge of his nose. "What the . . . Where am I?" A figure approached from behind, causing Ben to jump as he whirled around. He couldn't believe his eyes. "Sally?" She looked just as she had the day that Ben had met her in this very building. "No . . . this is a trick. I know it's not real . . . these hallucinations need to stop. Get out of my head, get out of my head!"

"Ben, you're awake! Calm down!" Ben pressed his hands to his ears, trying to drown out Sally's voice.

"No, I'm not listening . . . you're not real! Leave me alone! I'm tired of these tricks!" A new voice answered, ringing with a playful curiosity.

"Are you sure about that?" Ben pulled his hands from his ears, looking around.

"Huh? Who said that?" Ben wasn't ready for the answer.

The voice belonged to a man, at least as far as Ben could tell. The Entity seemed to materialize out of nowhere, dressed in a bizarre mishmash of patterns and colors. A purple blazer and lavender shirt with three black buttons, a crimson bow tie, purple pants, black shoes, and white gloves. The Entity tipped his hat to Ben, a horrid-looking purple number with black trim along the bottom. "What are you . . . ?" Ben asked, stepping back carefully.

"Tell me, do you recognize this place?" The Entity interrupted Ben's question with a question of his own.

Ben nodded. He recognized exactly where he was. "Yeah, the school. But, how did you—"

"How about your friend? Did you recognize her?" Another question interrupted for the sake of a question. This man was a real inquisitive one, as Badgy would say. Ben nodded, swallowing dryly. "We are in your memories, Ben. You see, I've been . . . fascinated by you for quite a while. You're unique, Benjamin."

Ben scoffed. "You're calling me unique? Have you looked in a mirror, buddy?" If the comment affected The Inquisitive One, he didn't let it show. "Besides, I'm just an ordinary person in this messed-up world."

"Incorrect," the Inquisitive One replied. "You're extraordinary and not like the others. You're supposed to be infected. You were attacked, back in Lucella. But you're not. You're alive. You're . . ." Ben sneered, but the Entity was not lying. Even if this was all in Ben's head, that just meant that it was closer to the truth. He had been attacked in Lucella, a swipe had come too close to his arm. He pulled up the sleeve on his jacket, exposing the small scratch that he had been concealing from the rest of the group.

"So what?" Ben asked. "What do you want from me?" The Inquisitive One grinned, even more offsetting now than before.

"Don't you see? You're immune to the Infection.

You have much potential to do things beyond your understanding." Sally reappeared from thin air as The Inquisitive One's voice cooed lightly. "I can help you see your friends again . . ." Ben reached out his hand. He knew that this wasn't real, that she wasn't real, but . . .

"No. I don't trust you. For all I know, you're just in my head, too." The Inquisitive One's eyes grew wide, nostrils flaring. Sally vanished as quickly as she had appeared.

"Are you rejecting my offer?"

Ben shrugged. "I'm never going to fall for any tricks you have up your sleeve."

"Hmm. So be it," snapped The Inquisitive One. "They're always stubborn at first. Then, when they have no one left, they come right back to me." The Inquisitive One turned as if to leave but stopped just short of the classroom door. "I have but one thing to leave you with; stay out of my business. If you continue to follow your current path, you will live to regret it."

Ben woke with a start, screaming into the open Doveport air. His face was wet, whether from sweat or the incessant pelting of cold snow on his face was anyone's guess. Somehow, they were at the mouth of the temple again. Ben didn't remember anything after passing out in the lower levels. He wiped his brow on the sleeve of his jacket, making sure that the material would not ride up and expose the scratch mark he had worked so hard to keep hidden. "Now he wakes up!" he heard Badgy exclaim. Whatever Spidella had jabbed him with was slowly working its way out his system, with the emphasis on *slowly*. It was still hard for him to move too quickly. His muscles ached with every slight adjustment he made.

"What happened?" Ben asked.

"What happened? What happened?" the badger repeatedly frantically. "What do you think happened? A giant eight-legged monster hanging from the ceiling dropped down on us! You fired a Taser shot—you missed, by the way, so sharp shooting there, Tex. Then you dozed off into la-la land. Me and Billy here tried to hold the thing off while Ollie finished the puzzle, but she had four arms for each of us. Ollie managed to figure out the puzzle and get the door open, but . . ." Badgy's voice trailed off while Billy kicked at the ground with his hooves sheepishly.

It was then that Ben saw Ollie. He was shivering for reasons entirely unrelated to the cold, his skin a clammy gray color. Ollie's shirt was slashed across the shoulder; Ben could easily see where the giant spider had gotten him. Stumbling to his feet, Ben made his way to his friend, caressing his head in his hands. Ollie was warm to the touch. Tears began to well in Ben's eyes and disappeared onto his snow-flecked face. Badgy reached into his pack and pulled a leather pouch from it, tossing it into the snow at Ben's feet. "I hope it was worth it."

"I'm sorry, Badgy. I—it felt so real. I was back at the school, in a classroom. And Sally—she was there. And there was a man, he—"

"So, it must have been Sally and the mysterious man who dragged you all the way back up here, huh? Do you know how hard it is to get two people back up that many stairs? Past that ax? You two are very heavy, and—well, I didn't personally do any of the lifting, but I'm sure that Billy's arms are very tired!" Billy raised and lowered his arms in a noncommittal shrug.

Ben brought himself to his feet, steadying himself on the stone column outside the temple. He picked up the pouch that Badgy had tossed at him and pulled the drawstring with trembling fingers. The bag fell open, bathing the bottom half of Ben's face in an eerie blue glow. So, they had managed to get the penultimate component without him. Ben smiled, nodding grate-fully, tears welling in his eyes for the second time in ten minutes. He pulled the drawstring shut, then looped it closed tightly, and stuck it in Officer Doggy's back-pack with the rest of the ingredients of the cure. For what he hoped would be the final time, Ben unfurled the map. The wind up on the mountains presented an issue: Each time Ben tried to assemble the map, a page would go flying into the caverns and someone would have to retrieve it.

A system of rocks as paperweights solved their prob-lem. The final component of the cure was in a military lab off the coast of the North Sea, the same body of water that bordered the island of Lucella. This final ingredient—Ben had never seen anything like it. The notes on the pages were full of jargon and sci-ence mumbo jumbo that Ben couldn't be bothered to figure out now. Ollie was the most science-minded of all of them, but he was in no condition to decipher anything right now. He looked worse now than he had before Ben pulled out the map; it seemed his condi-tion was deteriorating.

Ben tore a strip of cloth from his shirt, careful not to expose his bare arm, and soaked it in the snow. Walking back to his friend, he pressed the cool cloth against his forehead. He had expressed before that he had come too far to lose Ollie, but it was more true now than ever. Ben was carrying most of the components of a proposed cure on his back, and they had only one more to find. He thought back to all the close calls he'd had while on this macabre adventure. Ollie's house, the school, the police station, the gallery. All the running and fighting back he had done.

The temple, the military lab, the Metro station, the carnival, the grocery store. He had been struck on more than one of those occasions. If what the thing in his fevered dream had told him was true, he was immune to the virus. If that were true, maybe that was why all he got from Spidella's venom was a weapons-grade hallucination. Badgy and Billy had apparently sealed her behind the giant rock and smashed the wheel puzzle. Hopefully, they could steer clear of her web for the rest of their days.

The trek to the Doveport military bases was not like any of their other journeys. Usually, the quartet moved through the countryside as a unit, joking and laughing as they casually slayed their way through any zombie group that dared to attack the four of them. This time, they trudged forward in silence, snow beating and battering them into silence and exhaustion. Usually, they worked in tandem, someone always bringing up the front and the rear so that the group was always watching for the telltale glowing red eyes or unmistakable smell of one of the infected creatures. This time, they pressed on ahead with Ollie in Billy's arms, everyone's only concern being putting one foot in front of the other. Usually, they walked during the days and slept during the nights; the Infected were much less likely to be out and around while the sun was up. This time, they stopped for nothing. Day and night began to blur into each other as they made their way to the coast of the North Sea. For Ollie's sake, time was of the essence. Looking at Ollie, however, made clear that time was running out.

Ollie had always been small, even for his age; maybe

that's why the virus was spreading so quickly. His chapped lips were turning bluer by the moment. He was trembling in the cold as he tried to force out anything other than a low grunt. Ollie's face was turning steadily grayer as well; more and more color seeming to drain from his skin the more distance that they walked. His eyelids were heavy, making it hard for him to keep his eyes open. Still, his eyes fluttered briefly as Ben came near, gripping his chilly hand with his own. They were close; they were going to make it. Ben gave his friend a couple of reassuring pats on the hand as he pulled away, pretending not to have noticed the reddish hue that was beginning to encircle his friend's eyes.

Predictably, night had fallen before they reached the military base. The snow was worse here, perhaps because of their proximity to the North Sea, coming down in a flurry of wet, white powder. The Doveport base looked almost identical to the one in Lucella, quelling any fears the group may have had that they were misreading the map. Where in Lucella there had been a singular helicopter outside the lab, in Doveport, half a dozen trucks could be seen stowed away in the parking lot. Could this mean more survivors? When Ben's heart began to race at the thought, he hardly knew why. The people in front of him at this very moment were the only three people he had seen in months that had not immediately tried to consume him.

Ben pushed through the snow, now up to his thighs, as he waded toward the front door of the military lab. He began banging on the door with fervor; he was sure he would have hurt his hand were it not already frozen. Ben didn't know what he had expected, but there was no response from the inside. A blue glow to the side of the door caught his eye. A grid of numbers on a keypad; it seemed this was the best way to gain entrance to the lab. Ben sighed, removed his jacket, and placed it over his head to block out the snow and sun. The digits zero through nine were displayed on a keypad in front of him. Usually, this sort of thing was Ollie's purview. Ben preferred to sit back and watch his old friend do his thing, but his old friend was in no condition to do any kind of thing.

Ben shook his jacket, snow having already

accumulated in the hood, and pulled out Officer Doggy's flashlight. The keypad itself was lit from behind, but that wasn't what Ben was looking for. Ben shone the flashlight on the keypad, looking for which of the numbers may have been worn down by use. Now, he wasn't quite as good at this sort of thing as Ollie, but it looked like his choices were five, nine, three, and—Ben wouldn't get to finish his investigation. Billy, seemingly tired of waiting, had elected to expedite their process by smashing the door open, the handle of his weighted barbell sticking through the first-floor window of the laboratory.

Billy held the door open for Badgy and Ben before tugging it shut, keeping them from having to endure the elements any longer. Ben tossed his jacket on the ground, where it landed with a wet slopping sound. Somehow it didn't feel safe to be running around the lab with wet clothes on, and Ben had a sinking feeling that after all it had been through, that jacket might never be dry again.

This adventure had started in a lab, and it seemed it would end in one as well. Billy set Ollie down gently, tucking him away from the howling wind and pounding snow. This was their final stop and there was too much at stake to mess anything up now. But he knew that they wouldn't. Billy, Ollie, and even begrudgingly Badgy had proven themselves to be loyal friends and capable fighters. If anyone was going to save the world, it might as well be them. "Guys, I just want to say—"

Ben's potentially rousing speech was cut short by the sound of boots falling over tile. The trio turned, suddenly face-to-face with the entirety of the Dove-port militia. They drew their weapons from their backs, top-of-the-line stun batons that crackled and hummed with electrical energy. They pulsed a static blue glow, putting Ben and Officer Doggy's Taser to shame.

The Taser! Ben remembered his weapon, grabbing it from his hip and firing it at the nearest militia member. The electric barb bounced harmlessly off his body armor, falling to the ground. Ben frowned. Between the missed shot at the giant spider in the caverns beneath the temple and this, he was zero for two, and he had already used two-thirds of the Taser's charge.

"State your business!" shouted the woman at the front of the ranks, removing her helmet but not lowering her stun baton.

"Uhh . . . we're here to save the world?" came Billy's reply as if it were the most obvious thing in the world. Two children, a badger, and a bull show up on your doorstep. What else would you expect but the cure to the most dangerous virus the world has ever seen?

"Lies!" The woman spat. She seemed to be in charge, so it was to her that they would have to make their appeal. They were competent fighters, but they were one man down, and at least one of them had never tested his combat prowess against anything with an IQ over room temperature. "This is one of the last safe places on the island. And you bring two of them *here*?"

She pointed a gloved hand to Ollie, still huddled in the corner shuddering, and then to Ben. With his soaking wet jacket discarded at the top of the stairs, the scratch on his arm was now prominently displayed for all to see. Billy's jaw dropped while Badgy re-coiled in shock. The leader of the militia gestured to the two of them. "You two may stay if you would like. Your friends, however . . . I wish them luck." She gestured toward her second in command, and the man quickly marched over to a nearby keypad. He pressed a code in quickly, and the busted doors of the lab swung open to cast Ollie and Ben out. The wind howled and the snow poured down, each desperate to claim the two boys as their own. Ollie would not make the trip back to Lucella. This was their final option.

"No, no, no. It's not what you think. I'm im-mune!" Ben shouted as a last-ditch effort. He didn't know if it was true himself, and if they asked for proof, he couldn't very well say that it came to him in a dream. This time, it was Badgy's turn to drop his jaw. Ben winced. With all the chaos—getting poisoned by a giant zombie spider, Ollie being attacked, being held up by the Dove-port militia—Ben had not found time to disclose the details of his dream to Badgy and Billy. Even if he had, what if that's all that it was—a dream?

"Impossible!" hissed the militia commander. Ben stumbled backward, tripping over his own feet as the squad advanced. He fell backward, hitting the ground hard and scrambling backward until his back was pressed against the wall of the base.

"It's true!" Ben shouted. "It is a very long story."

Badgy and Billy prepared for battle, drawing their respective weapons as their opponents advanced. Billy's barbell was starting to show signs of wear, rust creeping over the weights and paint mostly flaked off at this point. Badgy's glowing pole looked as elegant as ever, casting a green light against the pulsing blue glow of the militia's stun batons.

The militia commander grabbed her helmet and fixed it back to her face, powering up her own weapon. "Now . . . by the power of the Doveport militia, we must destroy you."

"Must you?" Billy queried from the back of the room.

"You do that and you can kiss your chances of piecing the cure together goodbye."

The voice seemed to come from nowhere, yet still echoed off the walls of the base; powerful, authoritative, and firm. Confused, Badgy, Ben, Billy, and the members of the militia looked around, each searching in a different direction for the source of the disembodied voice. Ben surveyed the room almost frantically, already partially convinced that he was losing his mind.

Ben sat up, a small flashing light at his hip cluing him in to the source of the mysterious voice. He unclipped Officer Doggy's walkie-talkie from its place on his belt loop and pressed down the transmission button. "Oh, Willow. You don't know how good it is to hear from you." Ben was so relieved, he could have cried. When he fell on the ground earlier, he must have accidentally opened the walkie-talkie's communication channel. Staying pressed against the cave wall had likely kept the transmission button held down, meaning Willow had heard everything that had happened in the last few minutes.

"What's a girl have to do to get you to return her calls, kid?" came Willow's reply, crackling over the airwaves. Ben let out the weariest chuckle of his young life.

"It's a long story, Willow. I'll fill you in later."

"Mm-hmm. And that's also when we'll compare notes on the definition of 'checking in' . . ." Willow chided in a tone so strong that Ben could practically see the face that she was making.

"Enough of this banter!" shouted the leader of the Doveport militia. "The voice on your device said that you came to us with a cure. Explain yourselves."

"Oh, for crying out loud!" Badgy shouted, his glowing rod still raised high above his head. "It's the cure for bad breath. What do you think? We're here to whip off a big ol' batch of Zom-Be-Gone!"

"A cure? Two members of your party have been attacked and you come here speaking of a cure? As if it isn't bad enough dealing with the orange eyes, you bring the red eyes with you." The militia leader paced through her ranks, never taking her eyes off Ollie groaning and grunting in the corner.

"I know what you're going through." Willow's voice came over the wallow-talkie. "You want to protect your people, the same way that I want to protect mine. Well, let me tell you, this is the best way."

Willow's voice faded, and there was near silence as the leader of the militia deliberated, the only noise a dull humming coming from the overhead lighting.

"Let them through" came the quiet reply, but not from the militia leader. One of the soldiers had lowered their baton and stepped aside, creating a path for Ben and his friends. The soldier removed her helmet, revealing a mousy face and large round ears. She wore a bulletproof vest over a camouflage uniform with black gloves and white pants. Ben grabbed Officer Doggy's backpack and shuffled into the lab, not giving her a chance to change her mind.

"Mary?" called out the militia leader.

"I'm sorry, boss," the militia mouse called Mary murmured apologetically. "But if there's a chance, even a chance, that these guys have what they say that they do . . . we owe it to everyone to try, don't we? We owe it to everyone who's here. And to everyone who's not." Mary stepped back into line, demurely waiting for the tongue lashing that she was sure to receive. Instead, the militia leader only sighed, putting her helmeted head in her hands. "Give them thirty minutes," she finally relented.

Badgy and Billy pushed their way past a group of soldiers as the militia leader led them into the lab, where Ben had already begun removing the ingredients from Officer Doggy's backpack. In the back, three soldiers carried Ollie, each of them in full gear and masks. They were too close to take chances. "Welcome to Outpost Echo. You'll have to excuse me, but your friend is right. I have to do anything I can to protect my people. But as long as you're here, you'll have full access to the resources of this facility. Good luck, gentlemen." The militia leader shut the door behind them. "For all our sake."

Ben dug through Officer Doggy's backpack quickly, separating each ingredient and placing them on the lab table as neatly as he could. Normally, this sort of work would have been Ollie's purview, but with the virus spreading through the young boy more and more with each passing moment, it seemed the responsibility fell to Ben. It was simple enough to dissolve the apple seeds from the forest into the solution created with the chemicals from the school's chemistry lab.

Ben dumped the bag of glowing mushrooms onto the table. Billy used his massive barbell to extract every last drop of juice from them. Ben placed the liquid extract into a vial and inserted it into the machine. According to the Cure Papers left at the Lucella Outpost, the component from Outpost Echo was an isotope, a glowing green rod containing a not-inconsiderable radioactive signature. More interesting than that, however, was that it was one of two.

Ben loaded the first isotope into the lab's machinery. "Badgy, would you care to do the honors?" Badgy, who had been leaning against a wall anxiously watching the proceedings, snapped to attention.

"What are you talking about, kid?" Badgy asked. Ben gestured to the second isotope tray. If his guess was correct, it would be a perfect fit for the glowing staff that Badgy had been carrying since Ben had met him.

"What did your uncle tell you, Badgy? When the time was right, you would know?"

Badgy thought back to when he had gotten the large glowing rod he now held in his hands, and all the times it had saved his bacon from becoming bacon. If it could save even just one more life, then it would all be worth it. He gave it a final squeeze, tossing the isotope over to Ben. Ben slotted the rod into the machine, which accepted it immediately with a shrill whirr. That was everything. If the notes were correct, they were moments away from having a cure.

"You hear that, buddy?" Ben shouted over his shoulder to Ollie. "Just a few more minutes!" It didn't look like Ollie had a few more minutes. His eyes were fully red now and his breathing was ragged, coming in sharp bursts that sounded suspiciously like grunts. Every small movement the young boy made both reassured Ben that Ollie was still with them and scared him that Ollie would suddenly develop a taste for friends.

Ben took a deep breath. It had all come down to this. Lucella. Doveport. He had seen a lot of weird things over the past few months, but nothing would have prepared him for this moment. The moment it was finally all over. Ben double- and then triple-checked to make sure that everything was set according to the notes, then pressed the big red button on the console that he knew would start the process.

The button depressed with a loud clicking sound, the machine starting its process. The machine whirred and clanked, giving an obvious display that it had not been properly used in years. Ollie began to whimper, his eyes fluttered open and shut, and his brows soaked with an unnatural sweat. The machine began to sputter, the whirring slowing down. Badgy and Ben shot each other a worried look. They may not have known much about machines, but this was clearly not good news. The readout on the display gave the reason as a lack of auxiliary power, noting that it needed an extra 50,000 volts to continue.

"Is there a carpet in here?" inquired Billy. "Maybe I could . . ."

"Don't you dare finish that sentence. I don't wanna

hear it!" Badgy shouted, pointing his finger at his large friend. So this was it. Ben had pushed himself beyond what he thought he could, each time telling himself that he had come too far to turn back now. And now, now that he was nearly at the finish line, he was truly done. Ben fell to his knees in front of the machine, feeling hopeless. Badgy and Billy stood behind him, no longer sure how to help. You couldn't hit helplessness with a barbell; you couldn't outwit desperation.

Ben fumbled for the walkie-talkie on his hip, thinking maybe Willow or one of The Silver Paw would know what to do. His fingers closed around smooth plastic but not that of the walkie-talkie. He had forgotten that he had put Officer Doggy's Taser on his belt after unsuccessfully trying to bring down the militia member outside. He leapt to his feet, his heartbeat pounding in his chest, blood rushing in his ears.

After he had replaced the batteries at the grocery store, he had used Officer Doggy's Taser twice— once in Spidella's lair beneath the temple and once just a short time before. That meant that he had one charge left, and he was going to make it count. He was going to make it count for Officer Doggy, for Sally, and now, for Ollie. Ben held down the button on the Taser, electricity crackling as he plunged the device into the machine's power grid. The machine sparked, shooting little showers of golden light across the lab, but it seemed to have worked. The machine resumed its movements, the power warning on the display fading to nothing.

The militia leader threw open the door, flanked by Mary, who waved shyly as she entered. "Just what in the blue blazes is going on in here?" the leader shouted, her question answered by a small dinging sound as the machine produced three tubes on a tray, each filled with a colorful liquid. Ben, Badgy, and the militia leader each grabbed one in silent awe, holding the tubes to the light and examining them with a quiet wonder.

"So, this is it, huh?" the militia leader said finally. "This is the cure we've been waiting for. Of course, it will have to be tested in independent scenarios. We'll bring in medical experts, any scientists we can find who are worth their salt . . . There will be clinics, and trials, and double-blind studies, but after that . . . we should be able to distribute this en masse. Mary, get Sergeant Monroe on the line."

Ben loved the idea of government and scientifically reviewed medicine, but he had a different idea at the moment. Pushing past the militia leader and Mary to where Ollie lay gasping, he administered the cure to his friend. Ben tilted the young boy's head back, making sure he took everything. Ollie finished, let out a sigh, then closed his eyes, his head lolling to the side.

Ben waited a moment, then a moment more. Ben cradled Ollie's head in his arms, the silence in the room nearly deafening. Finally, it was broken. Ollie's chest hitched as he coughed weakly, rolling sideways. Color began to return to his face, and warmth to his skin, as the cure made its way through his system. Ben propped his friend up, watching the magical transformation take place before his very eyes. He hadn't seen many hopeful things the last few months, and once again tears began to well in his eyes. Ollie's own eyes flitted open, no longer that horrifying shade of red. For the first time since the cavern, Ben was looking at his friend.

Mary knelt down beside Ben. "Hi, Oliver, was it? Do you know where you are?"

Ollie looked around, even the simple motion causing his stiff body a fair amount of discomfort. "The floor?" Ollie replied, prompting a relieved chuckle from his friends. "Ben . . . where are we? Where's the spider?" Ollie asked, leaning into his friend to whisper.

"I'll fill you in later," Ben replied, hugging his friend tightly to his chest. The militia leader approached next, offering a firm handshake. When Ben took it, she clasped her hand around his, pulling him to his feet. "That was a bold move back there. Actually, it was a couple of 'em." Ben swallowed dryly. She was not wrong. "Yeah. Well, a friend of mine taught me about the importance of timing," Ben said, remembering almost fondly.

"So now we're down thirty-three percent of our

original cure supply," the militia leader noted. "What did you plan on doing with the rest?"

Ben thought about it but only for a moment. The answer seemed obvious. "We make more. Then we get out there and start curing people."

The militia leader snorted derisively. "Get out there? Please. Lucella. Doveport. You'd need an army."

Ben looked around. He didn't know how they did things in Doveport or how they operated at Outpost Echo, but from his point of view, he saw a lot of people running around in camouflage uniforms with tactical vests and electric batons. An army, maybe not. But it was good enough for Ben and it was a good start. The militia leader caught Ben's eye, beginning to catch his meaning. With the militia at his back, he could spread the cure across the islands and beyond, to wherever it was needed. At this point, he had come too far to turn back. "Well?" Ben asked of his best friend, his close friends, and the new friends he was sure to make. "What are we waiting for?"

About the Author and Illustrator

Terrance Crawford is a humor and pop culture writer from Detroit, Michigan, who lives in New York, New York. At the time of printing, he still has not received his Hogwarts letter.

Dan Widdowson is a children's illustrator from Loughborough, England. He graduated from the Arts University Bournemouth in 2014 and has been working on children's illustration projects with The Bright Agency ever since. With a keen interest in storytelling and narrative, Dan is working toward bringing his own picture books to life in the near future.

Turn the page for a special preview of another
AFK original story:

RESET DAY

BY CARLY ANNE WEST
ART BY TIM HEITZ AND ARTFUL DOODLERS

Scholastic Inc.

CHAPTER 1

"**A**re we there yet?" my sister, Delia, calls out as she kicks the back of my seat. She's asked this question maybe two hundred times since we got in the car on the drive to our new house, and if I hear her perky voice again—and feel her legs against the ridge of my back—I'll have no choice. I'll have to disown her.

"I don't know, but I'm going to need some serious massage therapy ASAP," I say, rubbing the spot where she punctured me through the seat.

"Pip, you're thirteen, not three hundred," replies Delia.

Mom, driving swiftly through some empty roundabout, realizes she has to play mediator.

"Girls, hold it together for another five minutes. We're almost there."

I groan. Mom has been saying "five more minutes" for the past hour. I won't admit it, but I agree with Delia. This road trip has taken *forever*.

I lean my head out the open window and feel the wind in my hair. The purple dye has faded to a lavender I actually like more, and it looks almost iridescent in the sun.

As Mom's car pushes on, the trees around grow thicker, almost like we're entering a different part of the world. And I guess, in a way, we are. When I told my old friends I was moving to place called Raven Brooks, no one—including me—had ever heard of it. I put up a stink about moving, but then Mom said I could dye my hair if we did, and, well . . . you know the rest of that story.

"I think I made a wrong turn. Piper, weren't we on track near that forest preserve?" Mom says, chewing the fingernail on her index finger. She keeps asking me to check the map app on my phone, but it doesn't seem to recognize where we are, either.

The fading sun hits the tiny diamond on her wedding ring, and I swallow the knot that forms in my throat. Truth be told, my position as "road-trip navigator" is new—that was always Dad.

Dad isn't here anymore, I remind myself. *You've inherited the mantle.*

"Mom, that wasn't a road. That wasn't even a hiking trail," says Delia, and for the first time in over an hour, I don't argue with her.

After all, it's not Delia's fault. It's not Mom's, either. This whole mess isn't anyone's fault but the universe's.

Thanks, Universe.

I'm about to restart the map app for the eightieth time when Mom races by a signpost covered almost entirely by a massive tree branch.

"Mom, stop!" I screech.

In a move I don't think even she saw coming, Mom jams her foot down on the break, lurching all three of us forward and skidding the car to a full stop in the middle of the road.

"What?" Mom demands.

"Uh, I think I saw a sign," I say meekly, and she eases back into the driver's seat, ignoring the tiny snort from Delia behind her.

"Sorry," I say. "I didn't realize you were so . . ."

"Exactly," Delia helps me out. "Nope. Not tense at all. Totally chill."

Mom reverses the car down the empty road.

There, as if hiding on purpose, is the back half of a

sign. I can just barely make out the "RAV" above the "OKS" below it. But once I do, there's no mistaking it—that's the sign for Raven Brooks.

Mom stops the car so I can get out and move the tree vine in the way.

"Hmm," I say, peering at the sign. "Get this. It says Raven Brooks: three hundred feet."

Mom shakes her head. "That's not possible."

I shrug and point up. "Tell that to the sign."

I have to admit, though—Mom's right. Three *hundred* feet? Surely we've been everywhere in that radius at this point. And it's all overgrown shrubbery.

Unless, a voice creeps in the back of my head, *it isn't?*

Mom sighs, her thousandth deep breath of our trip across three state lines. She sounds exhausted. I guess

I would be, too. We only lost Dad a few months ago, and now we're moving, and on top of it all, she's got to deal with me and Delia. Mostly Delia, of course, but me, too. The very least the universe can offer her is an easy drive to our new home.

I climb back into the car. If I had any confidence that Raven Brooks really was three hundred feet ahead, I'd sprint the whole way, letting the thick July air coat my skin as I ran.

As we creep toward the three-hundred-foot mark, Mom slows the car to a near stop.

"There!" I yelp after several seconds of silent searching.

"Piper, are you sure?" Mom says, squinting into the thick spate of trees crowding the road's shoulder.

"Oh! I see it now," Delia says. "Just under the branch of that big, gnarly one."

She points to a tree suitable for any nightmare. It has that knotted-twisted-old-oak look that just screams *I've been here longer than you, and I'll outlive you five times over.*

"How on earth did you girls spot that?" Mom says, leaning over me to get a better look at the alleged road.

"It's Piper, remember?" says Delia, and I can practically hear her eyes rolling back into her head. "It's her superpower."

My superpower. I cringe at Delia's words, but she's not wrong. I have a talent that's useless 99.9 percent of the time—an ability to notice what others usually don't. Or, as Dad used to say, I have the devastatingly boring gift of "observation." Mom says I have an eye for detail, but Delia characterizes it the way only a little sister could: She calls me Eyeball, which is maybe the most disgusting name to give a sibling. Except for Nose Hair. That's the name I've blessed her with. (And you can probably guess why.) I win.

Mom cranks the wheel of the car and rolls us slowly over the crunchy foliage blanketing the road. Tree branches scrape the top of the car, making a spine-rattling screech with every pass underneath one of the old trees' claws.

"Bird," Delia says suddenly from the back seat.

"Bird?" Mom asks.

This time I chime in. "Mom, look out for the bir—"

Mom hits the break. There's an enormous black bird standing in the middle of the road.

"Is it . . . playing chicken?" says Delia, snorting at her own joke, and I hate myself for laughing a little, too, but this enormous black bird is just standing there in the middle of the road, looking straight at us through the windshield like it's daring us to move forward. I'm not sure how much more bizarre this trip can get.

"Just inch up," I suggest. "It'll move."

Yet even as I say the words aloud, something inside of me doubts I'm right. I can't stop staring at the bird—its onyx eyes, its tiny fluff of feathers hooding the top of its slightly hooked beak, its oil-slick feathers pushed tight against its large body. This bird has no intention of moving out of our way.

"Maybe just . . . move around it?" I say when I notice Mom realizing the same thing I am.

"Around it how?" Mom asks, and I see what she's saying. It's hard to know where the edge of the road stops and the forest starts. Who knows what lies underneath all that overgrowth? It could be a six-inch drop, or some furry animal's habitat. Or some creepy bird's ground nest full of hatchlings.

Mom eases the car in a slow semicircle around the bird, tires crunching over the forest bed.

"Why does that bird hate you?" Delia whispers from the back seat. No one answers. To be honest, I'm not really sure.

Once we're past it, Mom picks up a little speed, glancing one last time in her rearview mirror.

"It still hasn't moved," she says.

"I'm sure it was just protecting its nest," I posit.

"On the ground?" asks Delia unhelpfully.

As soon as we turn left, there stands another huge crow, stock-still in the middle of the road.

"You've got to be kidding," says Mom.

"Do you think . . . it's the same one?" says Delia,

but if this is another of her jokes, none of us are laughing.

"It's not," I say, noticing immediately the distinct white feather sticking up from this one's head.

"This is nuts," says Mom, again edging around the crow in our path. "And not birdseed nuts." Again, the bird makes no move to fly away.

We're silent as we approach the next break in the trees, and when this sign points us to the right, we hold a collective breath and prepare for the crow that we're now sure will be waiting for us on the forest floor. Instead, the tree canopy thins, and what we see in place of the crow is a massive brick wall.

"What on earth?" Mom breathes.

I roll down the window and lean out to examine the wall, only to find it isn't actually a wall at all, but a sort of watchtower. I can see a turret at the top. Beside my head is a small metal box with a little black handle that says PULL.

Who am I to argue?

Inside the box is a tiny red button below a circular pattern of holes.

"I think it's a call box," I say, pushing the red button.

We're met with silence.

Mom leans over me toward the speaker anyway. "Hello? We're looking for Raven Brooks," she says. "Can you tell us if we're on the right track? We may have taken a wrong turn at the . . ."

"At the crow," Delia mutters. But that's absurd—there's no way that crow is a permanent fixture of the road.

Or is it? I think.

I scan the wall in front of me, looking for an actual door. Unless it's hidden in the mortar that joins the bricks somehow, I'm not seeing it.

What I am seeing, though, is the tiniest carving etched into the brick closest to the car tire on my side. I lean farther out of the window to get a better look, and what I see is . . . honestly, I'm not sure. What I am sure of is that I don't like it.

Someone has carved into the brick a sort of crude bird, except it doesn't look exactly like the birds that "greeted" us in the road. Instead, this looks like an unnatural cross between a man and a bird, standing on its two feet hunched and stooped, its neck sloped forward at an odd angle, its feathers hanging knotted and limp on long limbs that aren't quite arms but aren't quite wings, either. And unless my eyes are playing a trick on me, I'd swear that its beak is a set of teeny-tiny razors, ready to destroy whatever comes its way.

"I feel sick," Delia says behind me, and at first I think she's seeing the same carving in the brick that I am.

But when I turn, I see that she's pointing to a tattered piece of paper affixed to the brick farther down the wall. It says:

CLOSED FOR SEISMIC TESTING.

NO ENTRY.

"Huh?" Mom says. "How do you just close an entire town?"

"I wonder if this town was built on a fault line," I say. "Maybe it's earthquake-prone." It's the only explanation I can think of. Though I'm not really sure crows are so attuned to seismic activity.

I take another look at the call box. Mom's given up on it.

"Should we give it another go?" I suggest.

Mom shakes her head. She's got another idea.

There's a ditch nearby with a culvert through it.

"I don't like it," Mom says. "But we could drive through that."

"Aw, come on. What's the worst that could happen?" Delia says. "So we drive through a little standing water in a giant ditch. Maybe we get a little radiation poisoning. Maybe we get some superpowers out of it."

Mom takes a deep breath. Then she hits the accelerator.

"Yes!" says Delia. "I hope I get turned into a centaur."

"You're not going to get turned into a—"

"A radioactive centaur!"

As we reach the mouth of the culvert, it's a little narrower than I thought. The top has a lower clearance, too. With a bunch of our luggage latched to the car roof, I'm a little nervous about it all clearing. I wouldn't care so much, except my sound equipment is in the box strapped to the very top of the car and some of it was a gift from Dad.

I hear my metal case scrape against the top of the tunnel and wince.

"You know what'd be great to see on the other side?" Delia says. "Another creepy bird. Ooo, maybe my first task as a radioactive centaur would be to fight it. Wouldn't that be fun to watch?"

I have no idea what we'll find on the other side of the ditch. A road? Another wall? A raccoon in a top hat? Another bird?

All I really want to find is home. My *new* home, I mean.

Mom is a master driver, and once she's successfully navigated us through, we indeed emerge on a road.

It couldn't all end that easily, though.

Seconds after Mom stops the car on the other side, the roof that fought so hard against my case full of sound equipment groans loud enough to make my ears hurt. With a sickening twist of metal, the brick wall that formed the top half of the culvert begins falling away in chunks. The tin roof of the tunnel bows at a tight angle toward the ground.

"Mom, it's going to—"

Mom is gripping the steering wheel hard enough that I think she might break it. She takes one trembling breath after another, but she can't seem to breathe slower.

Or maybe that's me.

Delia, however, is turned completely around in the back seat, hands gripping the headrest.

"That was amazing!" she screeches. "Do I have an extra eye?"

Mom's eye is starting to twitch. Must be the adrenaline—I feel it, too.

"Mom, you're like an action-movie hero!" says Delia.

Mom doesn't peel her eyes from the road. I shake my head.

What lies in front of us is more forest, dense and thick. But there's a road that runs alongside the tree line, and that's good enough. *It's something to follow*, Dad would have said, and thinking about him here with us gives me a twinge of hope.

"Huh," Mom says, looking at the dashboard. "The outside thermometer must be off. It says it's sixty-five degrees."

Sixty-five degrees? In the middle of summer? That seems unlikely, but Mom's right—I'd instinctively turned the air conditioner off right when we pulled through the ditch.

Delia rolls down her window, and immediately, a brisk wind rushes through the car. But there's more than that. The smell is different, too. It smells like fall.

I peer closer at the trees alongside the road, and

while most of them are some form or another of evergreen, there are some leaf-shedding ones, too. And those leaves are the telltale colors of autumn, their varied shades looking like leaves on fire.

Mom commands Delia to roll up the window as we all brush away a chill.

"Just checking, that wasn't a time portal, right?" I ask.

Mom keeps driving. "It's just an unseasonably cool day," she says. "Must have something to do with all the branches. Well, that's fine by me. You know I hate the heat anyway."

But if we thought the weirdness was going to subside once we actually drove into town, we were so far off.

Driving into town is like seeing two different worlds—a thicket of wilderness on our right, and a fully developed town on our left. The houses that line the street along the left all face the forest, as though to watch it. Their yards are alternately littered with toys or adorned with crumbling birdbaths, well-weeded or carelessly groomed. There are two-story, skinny houses and flat ranch-styles, small boxy ones and wide, shambling ones. They all look lived-in, though

not currently inhabited. It's like we've missed the memo about a meeting or something.

"It is the middle of the day," Mom says, reading my mind. "I'm sure everyone is just at work or school."

But it's a Saturday in July. I seriously doubt that.

Mom drives until she reaches a traffic light, red

for absolutely no reason. It's not like there's anyone crossing, but rules are rules, so we wait.

I stare at a billboard that's towering above us. It's faded and shredding, but a billboard nonetheless.

It's got a picture of a bunch of kids, all dressed in retro nineties garb. There's a boy with a head full of messy dark hair and a wobbly smile and another with light brown hair. I can't understand why, but he has a sad face. It's like none of his features can pretend enough to make him look happy. Then there's a freckled girl holding a little rag doll, and another girl with her chin cupped in her hand, a dimple so sweet she looks like the stock photo that comes with a new picture frame. Then, all the way to the left of the row, is an image that looks like it might have been added later, judging by the more modern clothes and crispness of the image. He's the only adult, and his salt-and-pepper goatee and wire-rimmed glasses make him look equal parts smart and kind. I can't help but think he was added in later, almost like he were *just* pasted in a second ago. It's strange seeing them all together, looming overhead in this suburban forest town.

Then I see the text above their images:

"This is the longest traffic light in history," Delia says, and she's saying what I'm feeling, because all I want to do is be away from that billboard and this creepy spot.

Suddenly, a low rumble breaks our uncomfortable silence. I'd think it was thunder if there were even one cloud in the sky.

The voices are still too far away to make out, but there are enough of them to make a cloud of noise loud enough to ripple the air.

"Mom?" Delia says from the back, leaning forward between our two seats.

"I hear it, too," she replies. It's a mob. An angry mob?

"I think it's coming from over there," I say, pointing ahead to an area tucked into one of the residential streets.

"They sound . . ." Delia starts tentatively.

"Mad," I finish.

All of a sudden, the front door to a pink house directly to our left opens.

Out flies a woman my mom's age, with thick dark hair pulled into a messy ponytail. She has kind eyes, and a wave of calm washes over me . . . until I notice she's running toward our car.